POINT OF NO RETURN

A DCI HARRY MCNEIL NOVEL

JOHN CARSON

DCI HARRY MCNEIL SERIES
Return to Evil
Sticks and Stones
Back to Life
Dead Before You Die
Hour of Need
Blood and Tears
Devil to Pay
Point of no Return

Where Stars Will Shine – a charity anthology compiled by Emma Mitchell, featuring a Harry McNeil short story –
The Art of War and Peace

DCI SEAN BRACKEN SERIES
Starvation Lake

DI FRANK MILLER SERIES

Crash Point
Silent Marker
Rain Town
Watch Me Bleed
Broken Wheels
Sudden Death
Under the Knife
Trial and Error
Warning Sign
Cut Throat
Blood from a Stone
Time of Death

Frank Miller Crime Series – Books 1-3 – Box set
Frank Miller Crime Series - Books 4-6 - Box set

MAX DOYLE SERIES
Final Steps
Code Red
The October Project

SCOTT MARSHALL SERIES

Old Habits

POINT OF NO RETURN

Copyright © 2020 John Carson

Edited by Charlie Wilson at Landmark Editorial
Cover by Damonza

John Carson has asserted his right under the Copyright, Designs and Patents Act 1988, to be identified as the author of this work.

This is a work of fiction. Names, characters, places, brands, media, and incidents are either the products of the author's imagination or are used fictitiously. Any resemblance to actual events, locales, or persons, living or dead, is coincidental.

Without limiting the rights under copyright reserved above, no part of this publication may be reproduced, stored in or introduced into a retrieval system, or transmitted, in any form, or by any means (electronic, mechanical, photocopying, recording, or otherwise) without the prior written permission of the author of this book. Innocence is and

All rights reserved

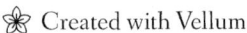 Created with Vellum

For Merrill Astill Blount

ONE

If Muckle McInsh hadn't had those few drams after dinner, he might have turned the Land Rover round and gone for help.

As it was, some of Scotland's finest product was coursing its way through his veins and he was more than up for a fight. He could have asked Wee Shug for back-up, but he didn't see the need. He'd already handed his notice in and the Wolf family could shove this place up their arse.

Right now, he was spoiling for a fight. He was more than happy to give one of those pompous bastards a tongue lashing. *Nobody is to go near the properties until they've been officially handed over.* Those had been the instructions, and by God he was going to enforce them. It wasn't as if they could fire him.

He could see the top half of the house appear as he

drove further up the private road.

It was the light on in the extension that caught his eye in the dark. Nobody lived in the house, and he wasn't privy to which member of the McTool clan had been left this pile of stones in the old man's will, and he couldn't give a toss, but he was raring to go now.

Sparky, his German Shepherd, sensed his anger and started to get agitated. Muckle laughed as the vehicle got closer.

'That's it, Sparky my boy. Get yourself prepared for a bit of arse-biting. And God help him if he has a weapon. Daddy brought the twelve-gauge.' He laughed in the darkness of the vehicle and smiled at the dog, who was now sitting up in the passenger seat, growling.

'Don't you worry, pal; if Daddy sees one of those shaggers is going to hurt you, I'll make sure you're not in the line of fire.'

The dog sensed he was being spoken to and wagged his tail.

Sparky was a good boy. Muckle's best friend. Yes, Donald in the pub was his best *human* friend, but his big furry pal was the love of his life. His wife came a close second for sure, but Sparky was the most loyal companion a man could ever hope for.

Why don't you get a sheep dog? Donald had asked one night in the pub.

Are you daft? Muckle had admonished. *What*

would I do with a dog who runs around like it's on crack?

No, Sparky was his early warning system, and Jesus was the end of the fight. He'd nicknamed his shotgun *Jesus* years ago, so if any bastard was causing trouble and asked the question, *Who's going to make me?*... well, Jesus will, fuckwit.

Muckle was disappointed that nobody had ever asked him that question. Probably because he was built like a brick shithouse and stood at over six feet, and the dog acted like he was inbred when he got going. Sometimes it took two commands of *Shut up, ya hoor* for the dog to listen to him.

It was obvious that nobody wanted punched in the mouth, shot in the balls or bitten on the arse by the giant of a man and his dog.

'I bet it's that wee arse-piece, Clive,' Muckle said as he slowed the car down. Clive Wolf, member of the Wolf clan and a royal pain. Nothing a good skelping wouldn't have taken care of when the wee bastard was growing up, he was sure, but they had spared the rod. Now, the young man sniffed stuff up his nose and drove his car while he was pished, thinking he could guide the car using a crystal ball or something. One day, that would be the only way his family would be able to speak to him if he carried on like that.

Muckle wanted to approach the house cautiously,

not boot it up to the front door and leave himself open to attack. Some people might think he was daft when they looked at him, but he would soon convince them that looks could be deceiving.

Still, you had to think on your feet at times like these. Maybe there were some housebreakers in there, raking about looking for a TV or the likes. Crime wasn't big on the island, but sometimes they got some scally bastard from the mainland hopping on the ferry for a bit of breaking and entering. Not that they would find anything of value in the house. The tenants had all been told to sod off after Oliver Wolf had died last Christmas. In preparation for the family getting what was coming to them.

Then the headlights picked out a bright-red Mercedes. The small convertible kind that people bought to impress others. The hairdresser's special.

Muckle scoffed. 'It's not even one of the big ones,' he said to Sparky, who barked a few times in agreement.

'That's enough, pal. I knew it would be that wee bastard. We don't want to give him a heads-up. I want to ask him what the hell he's doing here when there were specific instructions that nobody was to go raking about.'

Sparky barked again and stood on the seat as Muckle stopped the vehicle. Muckle's wife was always nagging him about not letting the dog sit on the seat in their own car, but this mud-plugger belonged to the Wolf family, so as far as Muckle was concerned, Sparky could tear it to pieces.

'Clive Wolf, baw-bag of the family. I wonder what the wee bastard's doing in here?' He put the vehicle in park but kept the engine running. Sparky looked at him in anticipation of some arse-biting, but Muckle held up a hand. 'No' yet, boy. If ding dong starts to give us his pish, maybe I'll let you have an early supper, but keep yourself together. And when I say, *Sparky! Get your arse over here!* that is not the signal to go and do whatever the fuck you feel like doing. I don't want anybody to think you're sticking it up me. I gave Donald a bottle of my best twelve-year-old malt to train you. I think I got the pointy end of the stick.'

Sparky stood on the seat and turned his head one way then the other as Muckle spoke to him.

'Aye, ya daft bastard, you know exactly what I'm saying. Tilting yer heid like I'm talking Chinese.' He reached out and rubbed the dog below his ear.

He looked out through the windscreen as spots of rain started to hit it. 'Magic. I forgot to bring my heavy jacket. If I get soaked and I go in there and that wee fanny is up to no good, I'll pretend I didn't recognise him and we'll truss him up like last year's Christmas turkey. How about it, boy?'

Sparky barked his enthusiasm, then stood looking out the front of the vehicle and growled again.

'I know, pal; who buys a red Mercedes like that? Apparently, Clive Wolf does. Maybe he's got a lassie in there with him. A bit of seclusion. But she mustn't have set the bar too high if she's impressed by that dump. Or him.'

The house, made of solid stone, looked like it was a hundred years old. It had been added to many years ago and was comfortable enough if you liked that sort of thing. The view was the money-maker; the loch sat below the house with the hills in the distance. It was secluded and private.

The tenant who had been told the lease wasn't being renewed was a businessman who had worked from home. Doing what, Muckle didn't know, but being head of security, Muckle had been called up to the property one Saturday night when a bunch of yahoos from the mainland had come over in their fancy foreign cars and thought that playing music at full blast was going to go down well.

Muckle had shut them down pretty sharpish after Old Man Oliver Wolf had called him. Even he could hear the music from the big house, and disturbing Oliver's sleep was not a pastime you wanted to get comfortable with.

The music had stopped and one of the friends of

the tenant had called Muckle a fat bastard. *'I might be overweight,'* he had replied, *'but at least I can go on a diet. Midget.'* While the other guests had laughed at the remark, the small man had taken a step forward. Muckle had let a little bit more of Sparky's leash slip through his hand and the small man got the message that he was about to become even smaller.

Oliver Wolf had found great amusement in the tenant's complaint about his head of security, telling the man to fuck off back to the mainland if he wasn't happy. Words were never minced by Oliver.

'Right, boy, you ready to go and do some security work?' Muckle had another glance at Jesus the shotgun and decided against taking it in. He'd need his torch in one hand, which meant only one free hand, and he didn't want Sparky running about loose while he had the gun. He left it where it was, within easy reach should he need to run back and get it.

Sparky bounded about in the seat. He knew he was at work, because Muckle had bought him a K9 vest to wear and the smart dog soon associated the vest with going to work. Muckle was under no illusion that his Shepherd was as good as a police dog, but when he was straining at the leash, people didn't stop to think the dog wasn't highly trained. They saw a mouthful of teeth on legs that could perform cosmetic surgery without anaesthetic.

Muckle clipped the leash to the vest, which revved the dog up. He opened the door, and Sparky was across the seat in a flash and he jumped down, starting to pull.

'Wait, ya hoor,' Muckle said, almost missing the driver's door as he pushed it shut without banging it.

The driveway was semi-circular out the front and Sparky made a beeline for the little area of grass in front of the house, where some bushes were growing in the middle. Sparky watered them before starting to haul towards the front door.

'Do you want that bloody bark collar on?' Muckle asked the dog, a threat his wife used in their house when the Shepherd became too rambunctious. As tough as he was, Sparky hated the collar and had soon learned to behave just by the very threat.

He stopped pulling so hard and Muckle made it look like he was in full control as he walked towards the front door of the house. He fished out the set of keys he carried on his rounds when checking on the properties. He looked closely at the front door as the automatic overhead light came on, illuminating the scene. It was slightly ajar, as if Clive had tried to swing it shut but hadn't put enough force behind it and it hadn't closed properly.

'Aren't *you* going to get a shock,' Muckle said, toeing the door open wider. He put his keys away and pulled out the Maglite from an inside pocket and held it up in such a way that he could bring it down hard on somebody, like a baton. There were no lights on downstairs and the sharp light picked out a little table in the main hallway.

Muckle knew he should shout out, but why give Clive a warning? He shouldn't be here, and Muckle wanted to see the look of shock on his face when he was confronted by one man and his dog.

Muckle wanted to check downstairs first, even though Sparky was pulling towards the upper level, where the light had been coming from. He didn't want to be taken by surprise, so he looked into the dark rooms on the ground floor, including the large kitchen in the extension, where the confrontation with the small man had taken place.

Nobody was there.

'Come on, Sparky, let's go upstairs.' He shone the light about as Sparky led him back out of the room, and they went up the staircase to the first floor. No light spilled out from under any of the doors here.

Muckle stood and thought for a second. He knew the light had been coming from a room at the side of the house, in the extension, which was a two-level add-on to match the original house. The master bedroom was there, at the back, a big affair with its own bathroom. That must be where the light was coming from. Not one of the other two bedrooms, used by the teenagers when the tenant had lived here with his brood. Little bastards, the lot of them.

Muckle didn't have kids and was happy with his dog. When he had met his wife a few years ago, she'd had a Beagle and both dogs had hit it off, which sealed the deal for Muckle. Love me, love my dog.

'Go and find him, Sparky boy,' he said to the dog, shining the flashlight around the landing and down the hallway that led along the extension.

He gave the dog a clue by walking towards the master bedroom. He stopped by the door and leaned in closer, not wanting to seem like he was spying, but he was security and had every right to be here. He knew for a fact that Clive Wolf *didn't* have the right.

He put the flashlight in his left hand, which was holding Sparky's leash, and put his right hand on the ornate door handle.

'Feel free to go at it, boy, if you feel we're being threatened.' He pushed down on the handle and shoved the door open.

There was only one person in the room: Clive Wolf. He was sitting on a chair in the little sitting area, illuminated by a small table lamp. He was facing away from Muckle and didn't move when the man came in with his dog.

Sparky started barking and not in a *Let's play ball*

kind of way. He pulled against the vest, straining at it so hard he was off his front legs.

'Easy, Sparks!' Muckle shouted. Then, to the young man in the room: 'Clive! It's Muckle McInsh, security. You okay?'

Christ, maybe he's pished and fallen asleep. 'Too bad if he has,' he said to the dog, who wasn't listening but was in full growling and barking mode now. The hairs on Muckle's neck stood up. Usually by now, the person who wasn't holding back the dog would at least show some interest in keeping their body parts attached, but Clive was out of it.

'Clive!' Muckle shouted, not wanting to get too close at this point, but knowing he had to. He walked forward, leaning back a little so the dog wouldn't pull him over.

Sparky stopped, the hair on *his* back now standing up. Muckle could see the red stain on the carpet under the chair. Then he saw the hole in the wall where somebody had smashed it with a hammer, the one that was lying on the carpet.

Muckle stepped forward and shone his light into Clive's eyes, a trick he'd learned to disable a person for a few seconds. But Clive didn't complain or put a hand up to shield his eyes. He'd never complain again.

Muckle shone the light at the hole in the wall. And saw the face looking back out at him.

TWO

'I'd like to propose a toast,' the elderly solicitor said, standing at the head of the huge dining table in the great hall. 'To Oliver Wolf. A man who was born and died on this fine piece of rock in the Atlantic Ocean. Wolf Island. A place you can now all call home. Oliver Wolf!' He raised his glass higher and drank the Scotch, then slammed the glass down on the table.

'Oliver Wolf!' the others chanted, all of them knocking back the first of many drinks that would be consumed over the course of the weekend. All except Shona, Oliver's daughter and the baby of the family.

And her twin brother, Clive, who hadn't bothered to show after yesterday's little tantrum.

The solicitor shuffled some papers and put them in the ratty old briefcase on the dining table, and then he closed it and picked it up.

'God help you all,' he said under his breath.

'Well, I don't know about you lot, but I'm away to have a squint at the property the old man left me,' Zachary Wolf said, tossing the keys up in the air and catching them with one hand.

'The old man must have been off his head,' Fenton Wolf said, curling his lip in barely disguised contempt.

'Oh, shut up,' Zachary said, standing back from the table.

'At least this place isn't crappy,' Shona said.

Fenton looked at her. 'I don't know why you're so happy; he left you that shitty little lodge up on Mount Arse Crack.'

'It has a nice view,' Shona countered.

'So did Alcatraz, but you wouldn't want to live there, would you?'

'Unlike you, Fenton, I came here to celebrate Dad's life and enjoy seeing his friends at the memorial, not blubber over who got what.'

'Why don't you just go out and mingle with the hangers-on and yes-men who worked for Dad then?'

'I reckon you ought to watch your mouth, son,' said Shona's husband, Brian Gibbons.

Fenton looked at him. 'You're an outsider, Gibbons, and the sooner you realise the dynamic of this family, the sooner you'll learn to shut your mouth and just sit and observe.'

'What did you say?' Brian felt his cheeks starting to go on fire, and he debated whether he should just lamp the bastard or have a word with him on the QT later on.

Shona's hand on his arm decided for him.

'Aren't you a bit old for her?' Fenton continued, the whisky fuelling his tongue.

'Shut up, Fenton. Good God, it's just gone nine o'clock and you're already halfway to being drunk. Couldn't you at least have pretended not to be an alcoholic until we all parted ways?'

'Sociable, dear sister. It's called being sociable. You should try it sometime. Unless you're too embarrassed to be seen out and about with Grandpa there.'

Brian got up and looked at his brother-in-law. He was about to say something when Shona stood up.

'He lets his tongue run away with him sometimes,' she said. 'Just ignore him.'

'Ignore him?' Brian said.

'I think we should just go to our rooms and look at the properties in the morning. We have all weekend.'

'Nah. I'm going now,' Zachary said, just as the door opened. A big man with a snarling German Shepherd walked in, followed by a shorter man. Wee Shug.

'Nobody's going anywhere,' Muckle said.

'Who do you think you're talking to?' Zachary said, curling a lip.

'I'm talking to you, dafty.'

'Cheeky bastard. You're fired.'

Muckle looked at his watch and smiled. 'I'd watch your mouth if I were you. As of seven minutes ago, I am no longer in your employ. So if you want to get lippy, my boy here will be happy to rip your fucking nuts off.'

'Aye, I finished at nine as well. Your man there will confirm that,' Wee Shug said. He nodded towards the solicitor, who nodded in agreement.

'So you can shove your job up your arse, pompous twat.' Shug looked at Muckle and smiled as if they had rehearsed this routine before they came in.

Zachary looked at the dog, who was now snarling and growling, sensing his dad was needing back-up. He didn't look too sure of himself now. 'What the hell are you doing here if you no longer work for us?'

'I just told you, nobody's going anywhere. I've called the polis and they're on their way up here. One of you lot is fuckin' deid.'

THREE

'I'm thinking about getting a tattoo,' Detective Sergeant Robbie Evans said as he and Detective Chief Inspector Jimmy Dunbar walked along the corridor to their boss's office.

'A tattoo? I thought you were feared of needles?'

'Who said that?'

Dunbar made a face. 'The last time we had a blood drive, you passed out.'

'I told you before, I hadn't had any breakfast that morning.'

'Pish. There were plenty of lassies there that morning, all giggling and laughing. None of them wet their pants.'

'I think I had low iron or something,' Evans said.

'Low self-esteem more like. But they're having a blood drive next month. You going?'

'Naw. I think I have something on that day.'

'Maybe I should just punch you in the face. You could donate blood that way, but they'd have to hose it off the floor first.'

'I'll go then, now you've convinced me.'

'You're going to call in sick that day, aren't you?' Dunbar asked.

'Faster than a bullet.'

'Fanny.'

They went through a set of swing doors and headed towards Detective Superintendent Calvin Stewart's office.

'So what makes you think you can get a tattoo without skelping your face off the tattoo artist's floor?'

'It's for my girlfriend. We just celebrated our second anniversary.'

Dunbar stopped and looked at his younger colleague. 'You've not been seeing a lassie for two years.'

'Months, Jimmy, months. This is the real thing. Hence the tat.'

'Aw, away, man. You've hardly had a chance to find out what toothpaste she uses, never mind getting a tat.'

They started walking again. The sun was beating in through the windows on the long corridor.

'What you having done?' Dunbar asked. 'Although I mentally kick myself up the arse for encouraging you. Let's pretend it's in the name of science.'

'Her name. I'm getting her name tattooed on me.'

Dunbar closed his eyes for a second. 'What's her name?'

'Bernadette.'

Dunbar burst out laughing. 'What body part of yours do you think will accommodate that name?'

'Well, not her name. I thought of just getting her initials.'

'If you're thinking of getting it on your tadger, that's all you'll be able to fit.'

'Hilarious. How would you know anyway?'

'*Rumours* isn't just a Fleetwood Mac album, son. All those uniformed lassies you hang out with don't seem too impressed.'

'They're just pals from work, Jimmy.'

'Keep telling yourself that. I've heard some of those rumours for myself in the canteen.'

They got closer to Stewart's office.

'It's a pity her name isn't Mum, then you could kill two birds with one stone.'

'That's not even funny.'

'So where is this tat going?' Dunbar asked.

'On my arm, of course. Bernadette Irene Graham.'

'Big?'

'What?' Evans asked.

'That's her initials: B.I.G. If she's notorious, then you're laughing.'

'Aw, Christ.'

'Better stick to Mum. I mean, that's the real love of your life. You still live with her, don't you?'

'Only till I find my own place. Bernie understands. She said she's quite happy to wait.'

'What kind of a place does she live in?'

'I've never been round to her house,' Evans admitted.

'She could be married with kids for all you know.'

'She's not,' Evans said, making a face.

'How do you know?'

'She told me.'

Dunbar laughed as they approached the office door. 'What do those muppets say to you in an interview room? *Honest, Robbie, I didn't do it.* And you just believe them.'

Evans looked past him at the door, as if the answer lay there. 'Crap,' he said quietly as Dunbar knocked hard on the door.

'I don't mean to pish on your parade, son, but check her out before you go emblazoning her name in lights over your manhood.'

'Come in!' Stewart shouted from inside. 'Oh, it's you two,' he said as he saw the two detectives come in.

'You wanted to see us, sir?' Dunbar said.

'*Wanted* is stretching it a wee bit. *Needed* to, more like. Sit down. You're making the fucking room look untidy.'

They both grabbed a chair opposite the boss and waited for him to carry on.

'You've heard of the Wolf family, Jimmy?' Stewart asked.

'Who hasn't?' Dunbar quickly looked at Evans to see if the younger detective was going to answer as well, but it was obvious his head was in another place.

'Wolf Paper. That's what started the ball rolling,' Stewart said. 'Then the old bastard branched into other ventures: Wolf Publishing, Wolf Office Supplies or some such shite. Old Man Murdo Wolf. Owned half the properties on Laoch, or as the pompous old sod called it, *Wolf Island*.'

'I thought Ulva was known as Wolf Island?' Dunbar asked. 'If I remember correctly from my history lessons in school.'

'It is, but that's some Norse pish. When those daft bastards with the long beards and funny boats came across here and started throwing their weight about. Old Man Wolf and his family named Laoch after themselves. But do you know what happened to him?'

Stewart leaned back in his office chair and looked at both detectives.

'You're up,' Dunbar said to Evans.

Evans looked at him.

'Have you been listening, Evans?' Stewart said, his red face starting to take on the look of an erupting volcano.

'Sorry, sir, I've been feeling a bit off-colour today.' *Unlike yourself.*

Stewart clacked his teeth together, mentally tossing a coin between going home and setting fire to his house or trying to keep his blood pressure down like his therapist suggested.

His therapist won.

'Murdo Wolf was having a party two days before Christmas, nineteen eighty-five. Some guests of his missed a ferry and were stuck on the mainland. So he decided to fly his own plane over to pick them up. The weather was shite, and not even Douglas Bader himself would have taken off in it, but old hardy baws gets behind the wheel or whatever the fuck it's called and takes off. He's never been seen again, him or his plane. Until now.'

Both detectives sat up. 'They found him?' Dunbar asked.

'Aye. Last night. The old man had been stuck in a wall in an extension that was being built back then. His grandson was found murdered in the room last night, while old Murdo was hanging out of the wall. I want you and Evans to get over to Laoch and take charge of the investigation. The Edinburgh crowd are going over too, since they need a Major Investigation Team on the island, and the four of you will be it. The forensics crew have already left. You'll liaise with the local uniforms. And you're flying over.'

'Flying? Business class, I hope,' Dunbar said.

'You can call it any fucking class you want. It's in one of those little flying crates that you couldn't pay me to get my arse into.'

Evans had gone pale. 'I hate those things.'

'You ever been up in one?' Stewart asked.

'No, sir.'

'First time for everything. Pack your bags and take plenty of spare underwear. Fuck knows how long you'll be there. There's some kind of family gathering and they're all there on the island, clucking about like hens. Go find out who murdered one of them.'

FOUR

DS Alex Maxwell sat in the car with the windows rolled down. The summer warmth didn't make her feel happy. The cemetery was peaceful, but the noise from the traffic on Drum Brae disturbed her thoughts.

She held the little bunch of flowers, staring through the windscreen. She had told Harry she wanted to keep her maiden name after they were married just for professional purposes, and he had been happy with that, and now here they were, three months into their marriage, and she felt a little pang of guilt.

Looking at Vanessa's grave sent a shiver down her spine.

The guilt stemmed from Alex being Mrs Harry McNeil, and the fact that it might have been Vanessa Harper who had married him if things had gone down a different path.

But she was dead now, Vanessa, and her mother, buried in the same grave, and Alex couldn't help but feel she was partly responsible.

She stepped out onto the road that ran around the small cemetery in a square loop, put her sunglasses on and approached the grave with trepidation.

She stood before the stone, not sure who was responsible for the marker. She hadn't attended the funerals but had encouraged Harry to go.

Now she placed the small bunch of flowers on the grave, reading the names over and over a few times. Then she stood back.

'I just wanted to say how sorry I am, Vanessa. I was stupid and jealous and I'm ashamed of myself. You were worried and I mistook that for you wanting to get back with Harry. I'll always carry this burden, no matter what anybody tells me. If you're up there, please see that I mean what I say. I wish things had turned out differently, I really do, but I can't change things. I hope you're at peace.'

Things had almost gone sideways with her and Harry. Alex hadn't told him that before she died Vanessa had sent her a text message: *You're no good for him. When he dumps you, I'll be waiting.*

The image of herself on her wedding day, walking down the aisle of the small church on the arm of Harry's brother, Derek, still gave her a pang of guilt.

Her own parents had refused to come; her sister, Jessica, had been the sole representative from her side of the family.

Alex had felt a touch of guilt even on her wedding day. She and Harry had talked about getting married for a long time, of course, but the events leading up to their wedding day would always put a tint on the rosy picture she had painted of that day long before she had met the man she would marry.

'Alex, sometimes you're a stupid bitch,' she whispered to herself. And the tears rolled down her cheeks, for her own selfishness, for a woman who didn't deserve to die that way and...what? Her parents' refusal to attend her wedding? She shook her head. No, it wasn't that. She'd come to terms with that.

Maybe it was just being in this place. Surrounded by dead people.

She jumped a little as her mobile phone rang, breaking her reverie.

'Jesus,' she said, fishing it out of her pocket.

'Alex? It's me,' Harry said.

'I know, dear husband. Your name came up on my screen. Talk about taking the mystery out of marriage.'

'I hate to rush you, honey, but we got a shout.'

'Whereabouts?'

'Take a deep breath and sit down if you're not already sitting...the Isle of Laoch.'

Alex took a breath and wiped the tears from her face. 'Where in God's name is that?'

'Off the west coast of the Isle of Mull. It's a little island. Population two thousand people or so. Somebody's been murdered. They want us to go over there with Jimmy and Robbie.'

'Okay. I'm on my way home to pick you up. I'm assuming they have a ferry service?'

'They have, but that would take too long by the time we got to Oban. We're flying over.'

'Please tell me British Airways?' she said, getting in behind the wheel of her Audi.

'I could tell you that, but I don't think it's fair to start off married life by lying.'

'Oh, God. A nice big luxury helicopter?'

'Yeah. Something like that...' His voice broke up and the line suddenly went dead.

She tried calling back through the car's system, but Harry wasn't answering.

She drove down Drum Brae and connected with Queensferry Road and headed home to their flat in Comely Bank.

Harry was in the living room with his holdall packed.

'Please don't leave me, Harry. I promise I'll be a good wife from now on,' she said, grinning.

'You wish. You're stuck with me now. Till death and all that. There's an empty one on the bed for you.'

'Boy, when you tell a woman you're going to spoil her, you really know how to do it in style. And tell me more about this luxury helicopter.'

'It's huge, luxury seats. But more on that later. We have to get going. One of the Wolf family has been murdered and they want us to get there before the small ferry gets in and people can leave.'

'They're going to stop them leaving?' she said.

'Not exactly. It's not a huge vessel. So they'll be able to note who leaves. But get a move on, love. Jeni Bridge already gave me an ear-bashing and the plane is waiting at a hangar at the airport.'

'Okay. I'll get going. Jimmy and Robbie will be there too, you said?'

'They're flying over.' He looked at his watch. 'Their plane is leaving in ten minutes. They'll be there before us.'

'Okay.'

'A patrol car is going to take us to the airport. Don't keep them waiting.'

'When have I ever kept you waiting?'

Sensing this wouldn't end well, Harry smiled and shrugged. *If in doubt, keep your mouth shut.*

The patrol car was waiting downstairs.

'The airport, son,' Harry instructed as he got in the

back with Alex. 'Private hangar down Turnhouse Road.'

'Yes, sir.'

They chit-chatted idly while the car sped along through Corstorphine, Alex looking up Drum Brae, where she had just been. She had been bracing herself for Harry to ask where she had gone that morning, but he hadn't. She had told him she had to run an errand and he hadn't questioned her.

The patrol car slowed at the entrance gate and was let through by an airport security officer.

'That was bollocks about a luxury helicopter, wasn't it?' Alex said as she saw the little plane sitting outside the hangar.

'To be fair, I did ask Jeni Bridge, but she laughed. I wanted to break it to you gently.'

'You couldn't pay me to go up in one of those things,' said the uniform in the front passenger seat. 'When they go down, there's nothing left of them.'

'Thanks for that, Sergeant,' Harry said.

Alex stood looking at the coffin with wings as Harry got the bags out.

'Fun weekend, you said.' She shook her head. 'You'd better have something good up your sleeve.'

FIVE

Harry was pale and his eyes were wide. 'We're going to die,' he said yet again, much to Alex's amusement. She was smiling, having the time of her life.

'The island is below us now,' the pilot said. 'The airport is on the south island. The north island is connected by a bridge, as you can see below.'

'Look, Harry,' Alex said, pointing out of the window.

The headsets they were wearing didn't make Harry feel any safer.

'No, thanks.' He closed his eyes. The sunshine outside didn't make the flight any more fun. If it had been raining and thunder, he would have slit his wrists.

'What's that on the north island?' Alex asked.

'Some kind of funfair,' the pilot answered. 'I haven't been over here in a while. Kind of reminds me of when I was flying over Afghanistan. God, I wish I had cannon fitted to this machine.'

Harry opened his eyes to see if the pilot was in a trance, and felt relief when he saw the man was taking them down.

'No offence, pal, but I'm taking the ferry home.'

'None taken,' the pilot said, and Harry felt the little machine fall out of the sky. But it was only on the approach to the runway. He was sweating buckets by the time the wheels touched down.

'There are scheduled flights out of the airport,' the pilot said. 'You might find a bigger plane more relaxing.'

'God bless you, son, but it's a boat for me.' Harry hoped nobody saw him shaking when he got out of the aircraft.

Jimmy Dunbar and Robbie Evans were waiting with a car outside the small terminal.

'They even have a wee control tower,' Alex said, pointing.

'Maybe we can send a postcard back home with that on it. That's the only way I want to see it again,' Harry said, lugging his holdall.

Alex swung hers and smiled when she saw the two Glasgow detectives.

'Hello, sir,' she said to Dunbar. 'Robbie. You don't look so good.'

'What a nightmare,' Dunbar said. 'Robbie gives a whole new meaning to *bring a bagged lunch*. The fucking plane was stinking. Even the wee lassie pathologist who came over with us got the boak. And she cuts people up for a living.'

'I told you I didn't like those things,' Evans complained.

'I've seen bairns have a better time on a plane than you.' Dunbar looked at Harry. 'You're not looking too hot yourself, Harry. Don't you like the planes either?'

'I just didn't get much sleep last night. The flight didn't bother me.'

Nobody fell for his lie.

'Right. We're not long here. The pathologist went to the hotel to dump off her stuff, then the patrol car was going to take her to the scene. The forensics team flew out early this morning before the crack of dawn. I got one of the uniforms to bring us a car and this was what they managed to muster.' He pointed to the old Mondeo. 'I'm sure they just bought it from the local scrapyard for us to use.'

'At least it's on the ground,' Harry said.

'Aye, that's all it's got going for it. But they've preserved the scene. Forensics have already made a start.'

'Where's the hotel?' Alex asked.

'In town. We haven't been there, but reservations

were made for us.' Dunbar looked at the others. 'Alex, you seem to be the only one who had a good time, so you can drive.'

Alex was looking across the airport out to the sea in the distance. The sun was shining off it, making it look pleasant. Behind them, hills rose up. She wasn't sure if they could be called mountains or not, but they were relatively high.

Dunbar tossed her the keys and they got into the car. They sat back as Alex started driving.

'Have you seen much of Chance?' Harry asked. His son had recently completed basic training for Police Scotland and had requested to work in Glasgow with Dunbar and Evans, rather than in Edinburgh with Harry.

'Aye, I have,' said Dunbar. 'He's a great lad.'

'Katie, his friend, would have joined him if it hadn't been for her mother being disabled,' Harry said.

'He's only an hour's drive away. It will be good for them. I mean, it's not as if they were officially dating or anything.'

'Dating,' Evans said. 'Who uses that term nowadays?'

'Shut your cakehole. For a wee Jessie who's just been squealing on the wee aeroplane, you would do well not to invoke a ton of slagging while we're here.'

'Anyway, I told Chance we'd go out for a pint one night soon,' Evans said, ignoring Dunbar.

'Just look after him, Robbie,' Harry said.

'Will do, sir. He's in good hands.'

'There're a lot of attractions on the islands,' Dunbar said. 'We were given a briefing, which I'll go over with you. We have a makeshift incident room in the station, which is not too far from here. I haven't been there yet, but I want to see the scene. We can meet the family first. Get a feel for them.'

'Sounds like a crappy game show,' Evans said.

'Even crappier when you think one of them was murdered. Just keep that in mind.'

'Aye. Sorry.'

'Robbie's upset because his holiday plans were cancelled,' Dunbar said as they arrived at the hotel. They pulled their luggage out of the boot of the car.

'Oh no,' Alex said. 'Where were you going?'

Evans managed to put on a disgusted, unhappy look. 'Tenerife. A week away with my girlfriend.'

'You sure you have a girlfriend?' Dunbar said. 'A real woman? Usually at the end of the holiday, you have to deflate her and pop her back in your suitcase.'

'Bernadette's real enough,' Evans replied, making a face that suggested he shouldn't even have had to explain that.

'Aye well, if it's any consolation, my weekend was

buggered too. Me and Cathy were going to go down to Largs with her old man. Now it's just the two of them and Scooby.'

'Jesus. Even your dug gets a holiday.'

'Never mind, Robbie,' Harry said. 'I'm sure your girlfriend will be happy to wait.'

'Maybe she's here with us now,' Dunbar said. 'You know, like one of those imaginary friends a kid has.'

'Can we just get inside, sir?' Evans said, eager to change the subject, as they looked at the outside of the hotel.

'The Laoch Lodge,' Dunbar said, shaking his head. 'No expense spared. I hope it's not one of those places you have to bring your own bog roll.'

'What place have you ever stayed in that you took your own bog roll?' Harry asked.

'Well, not bog roll exactly, but the wife and I stayed in a shitty wee private hotel on our honeymoon night and I had to keep putting money in the meter to put the heater on. I kid you not.'

'Why would you need a heater on your honeymoon night? Forgot your Wee Willie Winkie nightshirt?' Evans said.

'Why are your gums flapping? Besides, it was November. But it didn't look too different from this place. The owner was a miserable bastard. Looked like *he* laid the fucking eggs in the morning.'

'I'm sure this place will be different,' Alex said. 'It looks quaint.'

'Quaint, Alex?' Dunbar said. 'Is that Gaelic for *shitehole*?'

The building could have been somebody's house at one time, but now it was a small hotel. If it had any Michelin stars, they were well hidden.

'I thought this would be a no-name place,' Harry said sarcastically, some colour coming back to his cheeks. 'Mind and tip the concierge.'

They went inside and were met at a desk that served as a reception counter. A man sat behind it, reading a newspaper. He was older, maybe in his sixties.

'You the polis?' he said, putting the newspaper down.

'What gave it away?' Dunbar said. 'The fact that there're four of us or...?'

'Magic. The Fabulous Four, the travelling comedy act who moonlight as polis in their spare time.' He stood up. 'There's a reason the missus doesn't want any lippy bastards in here. We can do without your backchat.'

'What lippy bastards?' Harry asked.

'Those hippies going to the music festival. It starts today. Friday through Sunday. The longest three days of my life. They get pished and start fighting, but by

God do they spend their money. The wife won't rent any rooms out to them. That's why you have two rooms.'

'Two?' Dunbar said. 'Me and him are colleagues, that's all. Those two are married, so it's fine for them.'

'What do you want me to do? Let you bunk in with us?' the man said.

'What's your name?' Dunbar asked.

'Crail Shaw. But my friends call me Boxer.'

'Why's that? You used to work in a factory filling boxes?'

'Aye, son, just you hope you don't find out why they call me that.'

'They call him Boxer 'cause he's got a face like a dug,' a woman said, coming through from a back door. She looked a good bit younger than the man.

'Aw, nice, eh?' Boxer said. 'Just let them think a woman can talk to me any way she likes.'

'I can, you old fool. Bloody Boxer.' She grinned at him. 'But I love him. Bless 'im.'

'Oh, shut up,' Boxer said, leaving the reception area.

'I'm Nancy Shaw. I own this place, along with Old Torn Face there. My husband. He was right about those layabouts who come to the island every year. They use the High Street like a toilet and we don't have a police force big enough to deal with them. I'm glad they sent reinforcements.'

'We're not here for the music festival,' Alex said.

'I know, love. Clive Wolf got himself killed yesterday. Well, I think it was yesterday. I mean, I don't know for sure and I don't want to be a suspect. You know how rumours get around.'

'I do that,' Dunbar said, eyeing Evans sideways.

'Word gets around in a little place like this. It's put the wind up us, especially since it was one of the Wolf family.'

'What are the family like?' Harry asked.

'Salt of the earth.' Nancy looked at him. 'I know that's a well-used phrase, but it's true. Everybody calls this Wolf Island, because without the Wolf family, this place would just be another rock in the Atlantic. They live on the north island. That's where the big house is. Some of their smaller properties are there too, and they have a couple over here on the south island. They own the boat charter company, and the land where the music festival takes place is owned by the family.'

'What's the carnival up there?' Alex asked. 'I saw it from the plane.'

'This is the big holiday weekend, when the music festival is on, but the fairground is on six months of the year.'

'It seems like such a small place for a carnival to make money.'

'Oh, dearie, you wouldn't believe the people who come here in the summer. It's quiet in winter, so we make the most of it in summer. We have tourists all the time. Beautiful beaches, a lot of birds for photographers to snap, water sports. You name it, we have it. It's a hidden gem.'

'I don't think we'll have a chance to try any of it out,' Dunbar said, taking the key from her.

'I heard you telling my husband that you're just colleagues and don't want to share a room,' Nancy said. 'I have a spare room that's nothing more than a box room really. If one of you wants that? It's not a room I rent out; I keep it for my nephew. He can't make the music festival this year, so you can have it.'

Dunbar turned to Evans when he saw he wasn't moving. 'Go on then, Sergeant. Take the key. Don't keep the lady waiting.'

Evans took the other key from her. 'Thanks.'

'Dinner's included. Six till seven-thirty. I know you'll be busy, but you're welcome to eat.'

'Thanks,' Harry said.

A younger man came through from the back. 'Hello there!' he said, smiling. 'I'm Brendan Shaw. Nancy's my mum. The grumpy old sod is my dad. Let me help you up with your bags.'

'That's okay, fella,' Dunbar said.

'You sure? No problem. If you need anything, just shout. I just help out round here; I don't work here full time. But if you need me, give me a shout.'

'Will do.'

After checking in, they went to their respective rooms, but Dunbar just tossed his small case on the bed and walked straight back out. He knocked on Evans' door and entered after getting a shout. Evans had his case open on the bed. He took out a tennis racket.

'What's that for?' Dunbar asked.

'Protection.'

'Protection? You're a bloody copper. You've got an extendable baton.'

'I keep the racket at the side of my bed. In case of a break-in.'

'You'll be fine if Cliff Richard comes in wearing a ski mask, looking to tan your room.'

Evans propped it against the wall. 'That's much quicker than reaching for the baton.'

'I pity Bernadette when she's lying in bed with you and she asks you if you have protection and you whip out your tennis racket.'

'People have been mugged in hotel rooms.'

'I wouldn't know. We only go places we can take Scooby. Nobody would get through the door.'

'You should have brought him then.'

'Don't think I didn't give it some consideration. Cathy's old man will be feeding him fucking doughnuts. Poor wee sod will be double his weight when he comes back. I wouldn't mind, but I'm the one who looks after him. Cathy doesn't have to take him out last thing at night when he's burstin' for a pish.'

'You wouldn't be without him, though, boss, eh?'

'Not for anything in the world, pal.'

SIX

'A room with a view. What else could we ask for?' Alex said, putting her bag on the bed.

'Oh, I don't know; how about a swimming pool?'

'When's the last time you were in a pool?'

'Years ago when we took Chance to Majorca.' Harry sat on the bed and ran a hand over his face. 'I thought I was a goner when Biggles brought that pile of shite down.'

Alex laughed. 'I thought it was a thrill.'

'You said I was the only thrill you ever needed.'

'Maybe I'm widening my horizons.' She went over to him as he stood up and hugged him. 'You're the only human thrill I need, though.'

He kissed her and they stood apart.

'I wanted to discuss where I was this morning.' Her face took on a serious look.

'Okay. I'm listening.'

There was a knock at the door.

'Crap. Hold that thought. You can tell me later.' Harry answered the door and Dunbar and Evans were waiting.

'Ready when you are, neighbour.'

'Ready right now,' Harry said. Alex just smiled and they left the room.

Dunbar opened his phone and read out the directions to the Wolf estate.

It was indeed on the north island, on a road to the coast. A hill which might or might not have been part of a small mountain range rose up in the distance.

'Just point the car towards Krakatoa,' Dunbar said, pointing through the windscreen. 'Then left down to the sea.' Alex crossed the two-lane bridge and followed the road and the signs for the Wolf estate.

Fifteen minutes later, they were driving along the private road towards the big house. A parade of police cars were already there. A uniform stood on the driveway and approached the car as Alex pulled in. There was a large parking area in front of the house, with some private cars parked there.

Past the big house, they could see the ocean through the trees.

'Not a bad spot to have a house,' Harry remarked.

'I could see myself retiring here,' Dunbar said, as they got out of the car and walked into the large house.

A uniform let them through the doorway and they could hear a commotion from inside. A sergeant introduced himself and led them into a large living room.

A group of people were either standing around or sitting down. Some of them were arguing. A large man with a German Shepherd stood off to one side, a smaller man with him.

The big man walked towards them. The dog was wary, looking at the strangers, but Dunbar made a noise and held out a hand for the dog to sniff before rubbing the side of his head below the ear.

'You're a dog lover, I can tell,' said the man. 'His name's Sparky. And I'm Muckle McInsh. Formerly known as Inspector McInsh. This is my colleague, Wee Shug as he's known. Formerly known as Sergeant Angus Kendal.'

'That's enough,' the uniform said to Muckle. 'You're no' polis now.' He turned to Dunbar. 'Hasn't been for a long time either.'

Sparky growled, but Dunbar kept rubbing his head.

'That'll do, Sergeant,' Dunbar said. 'Just give us the gist of what happened last night. I'm tired, been flying inside a piece of metal that rattled like a bag of spanners, and if anybody here is going to be giving a reprimand, it will be either me or DCI McNeil there. Got it?'

'Yes, sir.' The uniform looked at Muckle, but the big man wasn't intimidated in the slightest.

There was silence for a few moments as the Wolf family watched the tableau unfolding before them.

'Well?' Harry said, starting to feel irritated.

'Oh, right,' the sergeant said, as if his brain had just kicked into gear. 'Right, McInsh there went creeping up to the house where young Clive Wolf was found.'

'Keep to the facts,' Dunbar said.

'He went there and found Clive dead in the bedroom. There was a hole in the wall, and Old Man Murdo Wolf was in the wall.'

A young woman in the room started wailing. An older man was sitting next to her with his arm around her. Dunbar would have thought it was her father had he not known in advance that it was her husband. Twenty years her senior and he looked every inch her father.

Dunbar stopped petting the dog and looked at the family. 'I don't know any of you personally, so I'd like you to introduce yourselves, one at a time.'

'I'm Brian Gibbons,' the older bloke said. 'This is my wife, Shona Gibbons.'

'I'm Fenton Wolf, Oliver Wolf's oldest son. This is my brother, Zach. Middle son.' Fenton looked down at his shoes as he spoke again. 'Clive was the youngest son and Shona's twin.'

'My name is Thomas Deal. Family solicitor. My assistant, Missy Galbraith.'

'We're going to need to talk to you all. I need you to stay here until we can visit the scene and talk with the pathologist.'

'Haven't we suffered enough?' Shona Gibbons said.

'Meaning what?' Harry asked.

'You want to keep us cooped up here. It's intolerable. I want to go home.'

'I can't allow that. You all have to be formally interviewed.'

'He's right, love,' Brian Gibbons said.

'Shut up. Maybe Fenton's right; maybe you *are* too old for me.'

Gibbons started to go red in the face and tried to pull her in closer, but she was having none of it.

'Get your fucking hands off me.' She stood up as if he were a stranger who had just tried it on with her. 'Fenton, I want to stay with you.' She walked across to her brother, and her husband looked at the two brothers as if weighing up his chances of taking them in a fist fight.

'You can bunk in my room, sis. Old Brian there won't mind. Will you, Bri?'

'Fuck off, Fenton.'

'Right then,' Dunbar said, having had enough of the charades. 'The two detective sergeants will organise the statements. You, Mr McInsh, will stay here until DCI McNeil and I get back.'

'I know the drill,' Muckle said. 'Whoever finds the body is the number-one suspect. Despite what Sergeant Bollocks there says, I *have* run investigations before.'

The uniform looked like he wanted to ask Muckle to step outside, but Dunbar got the feeling that Muckle would have loved nothing more than to give the sergeant a good belting.

'Nobody's disputing that. Just make yourself available. Give my sergeant your details.'

'You're not just going to let him walk out of here, are you?' the sergeant said, pointing to the big man.

'What do you suggest I do? Tie him up? He's not going anywhere.' Dunbar shook his head and indicated for Harry to follow him out of the room. 'Let's get to the house, Harry. We can see what the pathologist has to say.'

'Okay. You know where it is?'

There was a female uniform standing outside the house. 'Nope. But I'm sure she knows the way.' Dunbar called her over. 'You know the lodge where the victim is?'

'Yes, sir. You drive a couple of miles –'

'You know how to drive?' Dunbar said, dangling the car keys in front of her face like it was the first prize.

She took the keys without much further ado. 'Andrea Simpson,' she said after Dunbar made the introductions. Harry got in the back, not in the mood to be looking out the front window of any vehicle just yet, even one that was on the ground.

'You know the Wolf family well?' he asked from the back seat.

'I've only been stationed here for a year, sir, but I've met them a couple of times. Oliver Wolf was a really nice man. I was sorry when he passed away last Christmas.'

'Christmas?' Dunbar said. 'I thought it was six months ago? Which would have made it this year.'

'I think people generalised when they said six months. It was just before Christmas.'

SEVEN

The 'wee lassie pathologist' who had come over on the plane with Dunbar and Evans had a name. Dr Debbie Comb. She was just finishing up her initial exam when Harry and Dunbar entered the house on the hill.

Uniforms were there; one of them, standing outside, nodded to the two detectives when he saw his colleague getting out from the driver's side.

The sun was beating down, glistening off the loch in the distance.

'Not a bad place,' Harry said. 'If it weren't for the dead bloke inside, I mean.'

'Aye, this would be right up Cathy's street. Somewhere for Scooby to nash about in and all the peace and quiet she could handle. There's nothing like a night out in Sauchiehall Street to make the dream stronger.'

'I hear you. Lothian Road in Edinburgh is for the youngsters nowadays.'

'Christ, you're hardly a pensioner, Harry.'

'Anybody above thirty is old, according to Chance.'

'God help him if he calls me an old bastard.'

Harry laughed. 'He's been well-warned.'

Inside, members of the forensics team were walking about. 'He's upstairs,' one of them said through a mask on his face.

They went upstairs and were pointed in the right direction. Debbie Comb looked like she was barely out of school, but Harry supposed she had to be in her thirties at least. She had her blonde hair tucked into the hood of the paper suit.

'Dr Comb, this is DCI Harry McNeil from Edinburgh,' Dunbar said.

She smiled. 'The big feardie from Edinburgh? Pleased to meet you.' She held out a hand for Harry to shake.

'Big feardie?' he said.

Debbie laughed. 'Jimmy said your arse would probably have eaten its way through the seat by the time you landed.'

'Did he now?' Harry said, looking at Dunbar.

'Just making an observation, neighbour. Plus, this lassie exaggerates.' He held a hand up to shield his mouth. 'And she drinks.'

'Bloody liar,' she said, laughing. 'Well, we do go out drinking on a Friday after work, but it's not as if he and Robbie have to pour me into a taxi afterwards.'

'Not that you can remember going home, ye wee besom,' Dunbar chided.

'And here I was the one saying that Jimmy wouldn't be able to handle flying in that wee plane,' Harry said, warming to the doctor.

'Aye, he was hanging on for dear life. I'm sure he said a couple of prayers too.'

'Stop talking nonsense, woman, and tell us what we have here,' Dunbar said.

The smell of decay seemed to permeate every pore in the room. They became the serious professionals that they were again.

'It's a strange one this,' Debbie said. 'I'm assuming that the hammer used to smash the wall was the murder weapon. It appears to have dust from the drywall on it, as well as blood. And the blood is over the dust, so I'm assuming that somebody was using it to smash the wall and was then disturbed. But why would the victim sit down?'

Harry knew that nothing should come as a surprise at any crime scene. 'You had them leave it in place, I see?' Harry asked her, nodding to the hammer on the floor.

'I knew you would want to see everything in place.

Including the victim.' She nodded to Clive Wolf, who was still sitting in the chair. 'I know it's important to preserve the scene.'

Harry nodded. He knew that under normal circumstances the body would have been removed by now, but on this island it was important to have everything catalogued first.

'Crime scene have completed the photos and video, I assume?' Dunbar said.

'They have. They're just waiting for you to go over the scene,' Debbie said.

Harry surveyed the room. He had noted that the house looked to have been built a long time ago, maybe at the turn of the previous century, but the extension had been added around the time when Murdo Wolf went missing almost thirty-five years earlier.

'I don't think Clive would be sitting there and watching whoever it was take chunks out of the wall with a hammer. Then waiting for death,' he said to Dunbar.

'Makes sense.'

'Maybe he talked Clive into sitting down.'

'Or,' Debbie said, 'there was somebody else working with the killer. Snuck up behind Clive and let him have it.'

'That would make sense too,' Harry conceded.

'I wonder why they wanted an extension built on here,' he said to Dunbar.

'That's something we're going to ask them later.'

The head of the forensics team came back into the room. A woman who was in her forties. Dunbar knew this but wouldn't have been able to tell otherwise since she was covered from head to toe in a disposable suit. She lifted her mask and smiled at them.

'Hell of a thing, Jimmy,' she said.

'Lillian, this is DCI Harry McNeil from Edinburgh. Harry, Inspector Lillian Young.'

'Hello, sir.'

'It's Harry. Good to meet you, Lillian.' Harry nodded to the dead man sitting in the chair. 'If this was a game of Cluedo, I'd say this man was killed in the bedroom with the hammer. Not sure by whom yet, but if you could help us, that would be great.'

'Correct on him being killed here,' she replied. 'Dr Comb and I concur on that.'

Debbie nodded. 'Sitting in the chair. Blood spatter would indicate he was sitting when he was struck from behind.'

'The question is,' Dunbar said, 'how did this little situation play out? Did he come in here, sit down and get murdered? Or was he here with somebody else who was hacking away at the wall while he looked on, then that other person attacked him for a reason that we have yet to establish?'

'Whoever smashed the wall knew what he was looking for,' Harry said.

Debbie had a quizzical look on her face.

'Harry's right,' Dunbar said. 'I mean, what were the chances of him breaking the wall and finding old Murdo at that exact spot? Either he knew first-hand where the old man was or he was told where to look.'

'What about motive?' Lillian asked.

'Oliver Wolf died last December,' Dunbar said. 'The Wolf estate is a big thing to wrap up, I'm sure, but I'm no expert. The properties were divvied up between the offspring, and now they're here having a wee hooly to give their father a send-off. Invite family and friends over for a memorial, and then the solicitor can read the will and they can go and do whatever they like with what they were left. But one of them was left this place, and somebody knew about Grandpa being buried in the wall.'

'What happened to the plane, I wonder?' Lillian said. 'If the old boy was stuffed in the wall, then somebody had to have landed the plane somewhere. What if he wasn't even on the plane?'

'That's what I'm having my DI, Tom Barclay, look into. I'm having him fax over reports of the original disappearance. We'll have copies in Glasgow, since the family have their head office there and one of our stations was involved at the time. I'm sure the wee polis station here won't have any details on it.'

'You could always ask,' Lillian said.

'Oh, I will, trust me.'

Harry looked at the decomposed features of the old man peering out of the wall and he walked over to it. Although they had rotten away over the years, steps had been taken to line the space where the corpse was. It was obviously big enough to hide a corpse, but tight enough for the body to remain standing.

'Must have been awkward trying to get the corpse to stay standing up while the plasterboard was put in place,' Harry said.

'Not if there were two of them,' Lillian said. 'One holding him up, another one nailing the board into place. That's the logical thing to do.'

'Remind me never to come round to your place for a drink again,' Dunbar said.

'You make it sound like I'm your bit on the side, Jimmy.'

He looked at the others. 'I was referring to last Christmas when you had a wee shindig.'

'Of course you were,' Debbie said.

'I was. And if you think you're going to trip me up and get me to admit that Lillian and I are seeing each other on the sly, it isn't going to happen.'

'Just tell them, Jimmy. Get it over and done with.' Lillian grinned at him.

'See if Cathy could hear this talk now, she would take a nail gun to my personal bits. And you know how things get around. I don't want to be paying alimony for my dug.'

Lillian laughed. 'Take it easy, Tiger. Besides' – she looked at the others – 'Cathy was with him.'

'Harry doesn't seem convinced,' Debbie said, smiling again.

'Harry doesn't care what his colleagues in the west get up to in their spare time. But you have a point, Lillian. Unless it's somebody who's very dexterous, there could have been two or more of them. But is there any obvious sign of death?'

Debbie walked over to the old corpse. 'There isn't anything obvious from the front, but as you can see, I'm only seeing the top half. I'll be able to get a better understanding when we get him out of here and into the hospital down the road where I can examine him. I've been told there's a small operating theatre which can double as the pathology suite.'

Dunbar looked at Harry. 'He'll be given a post-mortem by Dr Comb with a couple of the forensics team assisting, as well as one of our sergeants in there to witness. Unless you want to go?'

Just the thought of being in a makeshift mortuary

made Harry shiver. He didn't do too well in that situation. Death he could handle; watching them being cut up, not so much.

'I'm fine with uniform being there.'

'What sort of time of death are we looking at?' Dunbar said. 'For the younger man, of course.'

'He was discovered last night around nine, which was' – Debbie looked at her watch – 'seventeen hours ago. I reckon he died within the last twenty-four hours, so around one or two p.m. yesterday.'

'Right. We'll let you get on with it, ladies. We'll have a debriefing in the station later on.' Dunbar looked at them. 'Where are you staying?'

'My team and I have a wee hotel near the harbour,' Lillian said.

'Me too,' Debbie said.

'We'll see you all later. You have my number.'

'So do I,' Lillian said, grinning.

'Don't start.'

He walked out of the room with Harry and found the young uniform downstairs talking with her colleague.

'You ready to go back to Wolf Lodge, sir?' she asked.

'We are that,' Dunbar answered.

Harry stopped Dunbar for a moment, letting the young woman walk ahead to the car.

'That guy Muckle McInsh said he came in here and found the body. We're obviously going to interview him first and his little friend, Shug. I'm not saying they look old enough to have put the old man in the wall, but what if they found out where he was hidden? We have to ask ourselves why they would want to get him out of the wall. Maybe they were being paid. Then again, why not finish the job? If Clive was dead, then why didn't they finish? Unless they were interrupted.'

Dunbar put a hand up. 'Let me stop you there, Harry. Muckle McInsh didn't kill Clive. I would put money on it.'

'How can you be so sure?'

'You know my DI, Tom Barclay?'

'I've heard you talk about him, yes.'

'Muckle McInsh was my DI, back in the day. He didn't want to let on he knew me. I taught him everything I know. He left to come over to this shithole five or six years ago. Oliver Wolf made him an offer he couldn't refuse. And Muckle's wife was only too happy to make the move. So trust me, neighbour, if Muckle had murdered Clive, he wouldn't have left him on display. He's far too clever for that. But we'll talk to him anyway, just for the record.'

EIGHT

'About fucking time,' Fenton Wolf said, standing up when the two senior detectives walked into the room.

Muckle McInsh was sitting down on a comfy chair, dozing. Sparky jumped up to his feet and started snarling when Fenton made a move towards Muckle.

'Easy, boy,' Muckle said.

'Aye, you tell that fucking dog,' Fenton said.

Muckle didn't even open his eyes. 'I was talking to you, arsehole.'

'You hear the way he's talking to me?' Fenton spat, pointing a finger at the big man, which only served to rattle the dog even further.

'Sit down, Mr Wolf,' Dunbar said in a tone that wasn't meant to be contradicted.

'Why don't you arrest him?' Fenton said, standing his ground. 'He's the one who murdered my brother.'

Now Muckle opened his eyes. 'Unlike you, dafty, I wouldn't have left a trail.'

'Mr McInsh, DCI McNeil and I would like a word,' Dunbar said, addressing Muckle.

'Can I bring the dog?'

'Fine by me.'

'We can go over the other interviews when we come back out,' Harry said to Alex.

She nodded. 'What a bunch, honestly. I'm glad I'm not related to any of them.'

Harry followed Dunbar, McInsh and the German Shepherd out of the room and into what rich folks might call a library.

'Where's your pal?' Harry asked. 'Angus Kendal.'

'He was here a minute ago. I'll give him a call.' Muckle did so and hung up. 'He was away to the lavvy. He'll be here in a minute.'

They settled down and waited for Shug. The small man appeared a moment later. 'I held off as long as possible, but when a man's got to go...'

'Sit down, son,' Dunbar said. 'We want to know where you were twenty-four hours ago.' He sat on a chair near the two men, who had taken a pew on a leather couch. Harry sat on a desk chair and twirled it round to face the room.

'That's easy,' Muckle said. 'Me and Shug were helping to set up the shindig for this weekend's memorial. Over at the hotel. There were caterers setting up tables, doing all sorts of stuff. It took us hours. We were there from around nine in the morning until about six. Both of us. You can talk to the staff there. The solicitor fella asked us if we could oversee it as Oliver's sons are a bunch of balloons. His words.'

'No offence, pal, but we'll have to check. Just to rule you both out.'

'I wouldn't expect anything less, sir. It's what I would do,' Muckle said. 'But the solicitor was there too.'

Dunbar smiled at his old colleague. 'How's life been treating you here on the island?'

'Pretty well. Until Oliver passed away. Me and Shug quit our jobs last night. We spoke to the solicitor a few months back, and he told us everything was going to take a while to finalise, but he asked if we could stay on as security to make sure the properties were safe. The tenants had been asked to leave and most were fine with it, and one or two gave some opinion, but they moved out. The houses have been empty ever since.'

'Did you work in Glasgow as well?' Harry asked Shug.

The smaller man shook his head. 'No. I started off life in uniform on the island here. I'm from here.'

'And you decided working for Oliver Wolf was a better proposition?'

Muckle looked at Harry, and Sparky perked his ears up, ever alert. 'Relax, boy,' he said and the dog put his head back down on the carpet.

'Let me tell you,' he started to say before Shug could answer. 'That laddie showed me nothing but respect from the moment I came here, but that fucking clown of an inspector treated me like shite. That kind of bollocks doesn't bother me, but Wee Shug here is gay. Nothing wrong with that. I couldn't give two hoots. In fact, he's one of my best friends. But that numpty inspector called him all sorts of names. And to his face nonetheless. I heard him being homophobic to Shug one day and I got wired into him.'

Shug nodded. 'Aye, it was getting too much. I mean, I can take a lot of shit, but he was getting relentless. Then Muckle came to me with an offer.'

Muckle nodded. 'I spoke to Oliver Wolf. Said I could do with another man beside me, somebody I could trust. That man was Shug. Oliver agreed; he'd always liked Shug. And when the inspector complained, I told him to go fuck himself and Shug was on the payroll.'

'Where's that inspector now?'

'Gone. He was emptied out by all accounts. Now it's Sergeant Turnbull in charge until a new one arrives. Turnbull is an even bigger balloon than the inspector was.'

'Aye, I'll second that,' Shug said. 'Turnbull is the worst copper I've ever seen in uniform, but at least he's not homophobic.'

'What are you both going to do now?' Harry asked, impressed even more with the big man.

'We'll find something,' Muckle said. 'Might even have to go back to the mainland. As sure as fate, those Wolf offspring will sell the properties they've been left and there would be no need for us anymore anyway. The hotel is right next door to this house, but that will go as well.'

'Right, son, we need to go and talk to our sergeants. We have to get some alibis sorted out.'

'You think one of those Wolf clan could have murdered their brother?' Shug asked.

'In my experience, when it comes to money, some people can't help themselves,' Dunbar replied, and Muckle nodded his head in agreement.

'Just watch that Fenton one,' Muckle said as they all stood up. Sparky was up in an instant. 'He's a fly bastard.'

'I'll bear that in mind.'

They went back through to the room where the others were waiting. Dunbar waved Sergeant Turnbull over. 'Keep an eye on this lot. DCI McNeil and I have to have a meeting with our crew.'

The sergeant made a face like he was about to say

something, but thought better of it. 'Just keep that big bastard and his dug out o' my way.'

'Aye, you wouldn't want him making you look like a wee lassie, would you?'

'Just remember one thing: we live here. You'll be back on the mainland soon.' Turnbull walked away.

'I swear to God, if he talks to me like that again...' Dunbar watched the man walk away, then turned back to Evans. 'Let's have a meeting in the other room before we head off to the station.'

The four detectives went into the library. Alex and Evans sat on chairs while Dunbar and Harry took the seats they'd just vacated minutes earlier.

'Right, let's hear what they had to say for themselves,' Dunbar said.

Alex had her notebook out. 'I started with Shona Gibbons and her husband. They were at the hotel the family owns down by the beach. They said that the staff there saw them and would be able to confirm they were there yesterday afternoon. They saw Mr McInsh there, and Shug. Effectively giving them an alibi. They were all doing their own thing before getting together in the evening. Clive didn't show and he was moody, apparently, so nobody was surprised. They didn't go looking for him.'

'Do we know who inherited the lodge where Clive Wolf was found?' Harry asked.

'Yes. They were told last night at the meeting. It was Shona. Fenton got the hotel where the memorial is being held, while Clive and Zachary have each been left a house near here. They'll each have a share in the Wolf family business and split the money. And this house.'

'Except Clive, obviously,' Evans said. 'We need to ask Thomas Deal, the solicitor, what happens to Clive's share,' Dunbar said. 'Who benefits from his death.'

'Maybe Shona, since she's his twin.'

'What about the other alibis? Like Deal himself and his assistant?' Harry asked.

'They were at the hotel as well,' Evans answered.

'Basically, all the Wolf family have an alibi?' Harry said.

'No. Fenton and Zach have hee-haw alibi. Out and about. That's all they've got,' Evans said.

'Do they all live here on the island?' Harry asked.

Alex shook her head. 'No. Only Clive did. He lived in this house. We don't know why he went up to the lodge. Shona doesn't know why. Her brother was strange. But no, the others live in Glasgow and Edinburgh. Fenton and Zachary live in Glasgow. Shona and Brian live in Edinburgh.'

'What about Deal?' Dunbar asked. 'East or west?'

'East. Oliver Wolf had a small flat in Edinburgh.'

'That's good enough for a start,' Dunbar said. 'I

think we should get them down to the station. Give them a formal interview there.'

They stood up and left the room again, going back to the living room where the rest of them were.

'Where're Fenton and Zach?' Dunbar asked.

'They left,' Thomas Deal said. The solicitor was looking tired and years beyond his age.

'Where did they go?'

'They said they still had things to do to prepare for the memorial service tomorrow. Apparently, it's still going ahead.'

'We need to ask you a few questions,' Harry said. He noted that Muckle, Shug and the dog were gone.

'Any time. But could we do it later? I need a nap. I didn't want to come here again, but there was a provision in Oliver's will that I couldn't refuse.'

'We'd like to get it done now, if you don't mind. Time is getting away from us.'

The old solicitor sighed. 'If you insist.'

'We'd like to do this down at the police station,' Dunbar said.

'As long as they have the kettle on. But I think I heard Fenton saying something about them going to the fairground. It's not far from the hotel. On the other side of the island.'

Harry nodded to Alex and she and Evans left.

'Our lift just went,' Dunbar said in a low voice.

'We'll commandeer a patrol car.'

'Why don't you use one of Oliver's cars? He actually left me two, a Range Rover and a BMW Five Series. They're only a year old, both clean and have a full tank. Missy and I are driving them back to the mainland. On Sunday, after Saturday's memorial bash. Tomorrow's Saturday, isn't it? I forget what day of the week it is sometimes. But yes, we'll be driving them back. Well, only one, as we have our own car. But you can use the BMW if you like? My knees aren't what they used to be, so it would be easier for me to get into the Range Rover. That would be okay, wouldn't it, Missy?'

'It would, yes,' Missy said, appearing by his side as if by magic.

'Fenton wanted us to fly over, but I told him, no thanks. So we drove. I didn't know about the cars being left to me. That was added in. Quite nice of him really. However, it leaves me with a predicament: there're only two of us and three cars. I need to find a driver before we go.'

'I need to find a lift eventually. We flew over and there's no way I'm flying back,' Harry said.

'Good. You can drive one of the cars back. How about the BMW? It rides like a dream. Use it while you're here. To be honest, I'll sell it when we get home. Not quite my style. I'm more of a Jag man myself.'

'I'm sorry, Mr Deal, that wouldn't be appropriate,' Harry said.

'I understand. Anyway, we'll meet you at the police station. But be prepared for a long visit. I have quite the tale to tell. Murdo Wolf did not lead a dull life.'

'You knew him well, then?' Dunbar said.

Deal chuckled. 'Knew him well? I should say so.'

They watched the old man leave.

NINE

'Come on, Brian, for God's sake. Make a bloody effort.'

'You might not have noticed, but these shoes aren't built for hiking. Neither am I, come to think of it.'

'Fat bastard,' she said in a lower voice.

'What did you say?'

'You heard.' She broke out of the woods, ahead of her husband, and he lost sight of her for a moment. God, she could be a real fucking pain at times. Still, he was focused on the end result. That was all that mattered.

He was well aware of the view from up here. They could look down on the building site that they had going. Luxury homes for sale. Luxury apartments. It had been a long time coming for sure, but the potential was here. A luxury marina was next. Yes, the current marina was okay, but when you started to get people with money coming to the island, they'd want certain luxuries, and Brian Gibbons was going to give those to them.

Of course, the other members of the family would be pissed off when they found out that Old Man Oliver had invested in the projects, but he had been a good businessman, like his father before him.

Brian stopped and looked down at the houses below them. Shona was staring off into space. Maybe she was thinking about her brother, or her grandfather. Brian couldn't give a flying fuck about either of them. The bottom line for him was getting this project finished. And when they could finally sell the house where Clive had been found, that would mean more houses to build. The land there was fabulous, with views down to the loch.

And Brian stood to make a killing.

He slipped and fell to one knee. 'Fuck's sake. Look at my fucking trousers.'

Shona turned to look at him, undisguised contempt all over her face. 'I told you to wear proper gear, like me.'

'And look like a fucking tree hugger or something?'

He could hear the music from the fairground in the distance below, round the other side of the hill, as he got closer to Shona. He bent over for a second as the stitch in his side flared up. He took some deep breaths. 'Jesus, I'm knackered.'

She did her head-shaking thing again, the one she reserved for when he was pished or when he'd left the toilet seat up again. *Cats might be able to swim,* she had explained one time in her most condescending voice, *but they don't like to swim in the toilet.*

'Profanity *and* blasphemy. You're doing well today.'

Here we go. Little Miss Uppity. Shona could be the perfect stuck-up bitch when she felt like it, but Brian had seen beneath the veneer. He stood up straight. 'I am. I'm absolutely fucked,' he said, just to push some more buttons.

'Oh, nonsense. My grandfather used to walk up the hill every day from the house. He said that's why he lived a good, wholesome life.'

There was something in her eyes; resentment. Yes, she liked the high life his building empire had brought, but the twenty-year age gap was starting to peel away at their short marriage. He thought she might be trying to kill him.

She ignored him and turned back to the lodge.

'It has so much charm,' she said.

'I'll have them put that on my tombstone.'

'Shona's starting to get a little bit ticked-off, darling.

Shona hasn't had her meds today, and Shona will be most displeased if her husband doesn't shut his biscuit chute and come look.'

'I know exactly what the view is like.' He knew Shona was hurting inside. The fact that she refused to talk about her twin brother's murder was one thing, but not wanting to talk about the discovery of her grandfather was even more disconcerting.

'Listen, I'm here if you want to talk about it. It might do you a world of good,' he said.

'Really? Good for me? To talk about my brother being murdered and knowing the killer is still here with us? How do I know it wasn't you?'

Shona's eyes were wide now, her breathing getting faster.

'Oh, come on, love, don't be talking like that.'

'You fucking keep away from me.' Now she was pointing a finger at him. Fight or flight.

'Shona, I think it's time we got back to the house. Maybe get the doctor to give you something.' He took a step towards her.

'Fenton said you were just using me. He knows all about you. He told me to stay beside other people. That you're dangerous. I told him not to be so stupid, but he pointed some things out. Like that place down there.'

Brian looked down at the new construction. 'The

houses? That was all planned yonks ago. Your father was excited about it. He gave it the go-ahead. How can you say I had planned this all by myself? Like I was trying to do something underhanded? Come on, come here. We'll go back.'

'Yes, my father planned this, but then he died. Two days before Christmas, just like my grandfather. Thirty-four years apart. Next Christmas the houses will be ready. Thirty-five years to the day since my grandfather went missing. Nice little fucking anniversary, isn't it? Fenton pointed that out.'

'Fenton's doing very well out of your father's death, though, isn't he? He gets a house and a cut of the business. He'll make money from the houses down there because your father invested. Don't you see how backward his thinking is? I know everybody's emotions are running high, but don't let your thinking get warped.' He reached a hand out for her, but she just took two steps away from him.

'Clive never trusted you, did you know that?'

'What are you saying?' Brian asked.

'He told me he wanted to show me something. He knew something nobody else did. He overheard somebody talking about where my grandfather was hidden.'

'That doesn't make sense.'

'You knew too, didn't you?'

Brian took another step towards her, holding out a hand for her to take. She took another step away from him.

'I don't know what you're talking about,' he said, his eyes piercing into hers. The sun was above, bouncing off the sea in the distance. Music from the carnival floated up to them on the hillside. They couldn't see it, but it could be heard.

'Clive made a will. He was paranoid after my dad died. Clive said he was murdered, just like Grandfather. How he knew Grandfather was murdered, I don't know. But he made a will, leaving everything to me if he should die. We all knew what property we were getting, but it was my father's wish that we only got the keys to the properties at the memorial. Clive said there was method in his madness. He told me not to trust you. You and my brothers. Now I hate you all. I'm going to talk to the police.'

'Oh, yeah?' Brian said. 'And tell them what then?' He was starting to get pissed-off with her now.

'Wouldn't you like to know?'

'I would, yes.' He was sweating now and he took a cotton hanky out of a back pocket and wiped his forehead.

'Look at you,' Shona said, her lip curling in disgust.

'Why did you marry me if I disgust you?'

'You were a friend of my father's. The boys would tease me about being left on the shelf. My first marriage didn't work out. I was lonely. Foolish too, obviously. You were rich, though, or so I thought. Fuck knows I wasn't attracted to you physically. Little did I know you were mortgaged up to the hilt. You're all fucking piss and wind. But guess what? This charade is over. We're getting a divorce. I don't need you now.'

'This is insane, Shona. I love you.' He didn't want to sound like he was pleading, but it started to come out like that.

'Oh, fuck off. I don't love you. Never have. I can't believe it at times. All my friends said I could do better. *Marry somebody younger,* they said. I should have listened.'

'You're being irrational,' Brian said, his breath coming in rasps.

'Jesus, you sound like you're going to pop your fucking clogs. I hope you do. Old bastard.'

She turned and started walking in the opposite direction from him, back towards their car, and then she *felt*, rather than heard, him gaining on her. Maybe it was the thumping of his feet on the hard, dry ground or his laboured breathing, but whatever it was, it made her turn round. And the big, steaming hulk of her husband was catching up. Probably because they were heading downhill now. It had to be. The bastard would die if they were going uphill.

She let out a yelp, just for a second, then she composed herself. It was thatmomenthere a woman who was about to be attacked could go in one of two directions: panic and die, or fight and run.

Shona was running. The fight might be avoided. Of course she felt the fear inside. She'd never seen her husband like this before, but the look on his face wasn't an invitation to have tea.

She was on a direct path down to the building site. The houses would have views of the hill on one side and the new marina on the other, when it was completed.

This was a well-worn path she was on. She'd known it was here as she'd climbed here many times when growing up. Old Huff and Puff knew fuck all about this island, except where to spend money.

Her father's money!

Bastard.

Although they had come up this way, sometimes when you went somewhere, it looked completely different in reverse. She hoped Brian would get confused and lost.

She kept on running. Aware that Brian could trip and fall and come barrelling down the hill on top of her, she risked a quick look over her shoulder.

He was lagging behind, and the coronary that had

his name on it looked like it was coming to collect. His face was beetroot, his arms flailing about like he was about to go head over arse down the hill.

She rounded a corner and was out of his sight. A few minutes later, when she looked back, he was nowhere to be seen. Running wasn't Brian's thing. Hopefully, he had given up, realising if he followed her down here, he would have further to walk home. He'd probably turned and gone back, so he could make it down the other side and call for somebody to pick him up.

She took her phone out. There were no bars out this far. They were working on getting a new tower up, but not fast enough, obviously.

Shona came through a line of trees, and a few minutes later she was at the bottom, her boots crunching across a gravel car park, the grey stones spoiling what had once been a lush, green park. 'Plenty of parks on the islands,' Brian had said. 'People need houses, somewhere to sleep. To entertain. To stay while they're having a good time.'

She ran across the gravel towards their car. Not the flashy new one from back home, but the shitey old Volvo that Brian insisted on driving while they were up here.

'If the bastards want something and break into it, they'll find fuck all,' he said. Maybe he was right, but it didn't matter because the old estate car was waiting for her on the edge of the building site.

Her breath was starting to tear at her lungs now and her legs were starting to burn. She looked round and Roly-poly was nowhere to be seen.

She got the keys out, keeping a firm grip on them. This wasn't a pathetic film where the daft lassie drops her keys and the vampire steps round the car and bites her. The key was into the lock in one smooth motion and the door was open.

The engine started first time. There was a big JCB in front of her, a few car lengths away. She squinted through the windscreen at the cab of the big yellow machine as its engine revved hard and black smoke chugged out of its exhaust.

It was facing away from her, its back bucket suspended in the air like a cat that had lifted a paw and was about to strike.

Before she could wonder any more, the machine was moving towards her, the bucket rising fast. She panicked and put the car into reverse, but it stalled.

She looked up and saw the machine coming closer. Her last thought on earth was of her dad. She shouted out for him in the confines of the car, knowing she wasn't going to get away.

The metal sliced through the windscreen of the

car, ripping away the A pillar on the side, and ended Shona Gibbons' life.

TEN

Thomas Deal leaned back in the chair and smacked his lips together. 'Damn fine cup of tea that.'

'Glad you enjoyed it,' Harry said to him. Dunbar was making notes on a pad. This station didn't have a camera recording system, nor an audio system for that matter.

What they did have was an old tape recorder that Dunbar had asked about, assuming it had been rejected by Noah before embarking on his trip on the ark.

The room was small, with a window set up high. The beige walls had scrapes on them like battle scars. There was a stale smell about the room, as if nobody had been questioned in here since the Kray Twins ruled London.

'Right then, Mr Deal,' Dunbar said, putting his pen

down and looking at the old man. 'We need to know why somebody would want Clive Wolf dead.'

'I agree, but where to begin? I haven't a clue.'

'You were the family solicitor in all personal matters?' Harry asked. Already his back was starting to bother him, and his arse was about to follow suit. The chairs in this little room had been found by a surly uniform who looked like he could have carried them on his forehead.

'I am indeed.' Deal sat up again. 'I am totally shocked by Clive's death.'

'Did Clive leave a will that you know of?' Harry fidgeted in his chair.

'Yes. He left everything to Shona. Now that he's dead, I will have to execute that will.'

'Did Shona know that she was the beneficiary?' Dunbar asked.

'I haven't a clue. If she did, she didn't hear it from me.'

'Did Clive Wolf have enemies?'

'Not that I'm aware of. He lived here on the island, in the big house with his father, before Oliver passed on. He ran the hotel. It was a simple life, but he enjoyed it. I can't think of anybody who would have wanted to harm him.'

'The problem we have,' Harry said, 'is this: did Clive interrupt somebody who was breaking the wall to uncover old Murdo, or was he doing it, and somebody else interrupted him and killed him?'

'I can see the predicament.'

'If it was Clive who was there breaking the wall, how did he know old Murdo was buried there?' Dunbar said.

Deal hung his head for a second before looking at both men. 'I was a young man back when Murdo disappeared. I was good friends with Oliver. He was only two years older than me. We'd met at university; hit it off right away. I became a friend of the family after that, and Murdo welcomed me with open arms, especially since my own father was dead. When he disappeared that night, Oliver and I were both gutted. It was unreal. The kids were little, all of them under the age of ten.'

'Do you remember what happened that night?' Harry asked.

'Like it was yesterday,' Deal answered.

'Why don't you tell us about it.'

Thomas Deal looked past the two detectives for a moment, staring at the wall as if a film were being shown there.

'Everyone was excited about Christmas...'

ELEVEN

1985

'OH, bugger, it's a cold one, alright,' Murdo Wolf said, rubbing his hands in front of the log fire in the great room. 'Where's that lazy bastard with the wood?'

Oliver Wolf, his son, sat in one of the luxurious leather wing chairs with his friend, Thomas Deal, on the other side, each of them straddling the large fireplace, a drink in their hand.

'Is that a hypothetical question?' Oliver said.

'No, it bloody well isn't,' the old man snapped. They all looked as the door at the side of the fireplace opened and Crail Shaw came in with an armful of wood.

'Boxer! Where the hell have you been? I'm freezing!' Murdo said, his face contorting into a look of disgust. 'Is that what I pay you for? To slack off? Get those bloody logs on the fire. It's already dark and I don't want this place getting cold while we're over at the hotel.'

'Yes, sir. Sorry, sir,' Boxer said, walking forward with the wood. He knelt down and began putting the logs onto the flames, sparks spitting back out at him.

Murdo stepped back and addressed his son again. 'The guests will be getting ready for dinner. We should get over there. Are you fit, Thomas?'

'I'm raring to go, sir.'

'Good man! My son is a lightweight when it comes to drinking. Maybe a good steak inside of him will fill him up enough to make him go the full night without falling over. What say you, Oliver? Think you can drink like a man tonight instead of some pansy?'

'For God's sake. This is not dinner with the Borgias.'

'No, but I've invited my friends over from Glasgow and I don't want them seeing my son flopping about trying not to puke over his shoes.'

'You would think I was sixteen again, not a thirty-two-year-old man with a family,' Oliver said.

'Some people never rise up to the Wolf mantle. I'm

afraid to say, my son is one of them,' Murdo said. He turned to face Boxer again. 'Unlike this fine young man. He was out in the blowing snow, getting us wood. That's a real man. Good job there, my friend.'

'Thank you, sir.'

'There will be a hefty bonus for Christmas.'

'There's no need, sir,' Boxer said, standing up.

'Of course there is. You work for me. That makes you family.' Murdo smiled at his son, but there was only malice there. He had made the comment to Boxer just to rile his son.

'Come on, let's get along to the hotel.' He turned to Boxer again. 'Bring the family, Crail. I'd like to see your wife again. And those little boys of yours. How old are they now?'

'Just turned five months, sir.'

'Bring them along, have some dinner with us. There's going to be a lot of people there.'

'I think the wife is going to be putting the babies to bed shortly.'

'Okay then, my friend. But you bring them around here any time. You're always welcome here.'

'I will, sir, thank you.'

'Right,' Murdo said to Oliver, and he threw back the remains of the whisky in his glass. 'Let's get moving. This is going to be one night you're not going to forget.'

The car was waiting outside. Murdo's wife had been dead for two years and he felt it at this time of year. Birthdays too, but that was more personal.. Christmas was a family thing, and he felt her absence more with each passing year.

The hotel was down a snow-covered road. Boxer was driving the lead car. He was a driver for the family, amongst other things. The wheels slipped but Boxer kept control.

'See that lad? Keeping it together,' Murdo said.

Oliver and Deal were sitting in the back of the big car.

'It's not a long drive,' Oliver replied.

'And? You would have had us through a fucking hedge. Boxer there is the main man. Eh, son?' Murdo smiled at Boxer, who didn't reply but kept his eyes on the road ahead.

They turned into the big car park at the front of the hotel. Christmas lights were on a tree at the front window and strung across the façade.

'Beautiful. I love this place. There's nowhere else like it on this earth,' Murdo said to no one in particular.

They got out of the warmth into the falling snow. Whoever had ploughed the front had done a good job, but the snow was coming down faster than anybody could keep it clear.

'Right, let's get inside. And remember, Oliver: try to keep it together, son.'

Oliver and Deal followed the old man into the hotel. Boxer parked the car and followed them in. They shook off the little bit of snow that had fallen on them.

'Now, then, where're my friends?' Murdo said as the hotel manager came across to greet them.

'This way, sir. In the ballroom.'

The room was filled with people, while a band played at one end. The drinks were flowing, there was a buffet set up and the guests were all having a good time, with Murdo footing the bill.

They were pleased to see him.

'Drunken old sod,' Oliver said.

'Don't take it to heart, old friend,' said Deal. 'You know what your father is like. Besides, he's not had that much to drink.'

'Enough to make his mouth rattle.'

'Come on, I think I see a couple of women we know. Let's have a dance and something to eat. I'm going to enjoy myself.'

While Oliver and Deal went to talk to their friends, Murdo was pulled aside by the hotel manager.

'Sorry to interrupt, sir, but two of your guests can't make it. The ferry was cancelled and they're stuck in Oban.'

'What?' Murdo said, his voice just a little too loud. 'Who is it?'

'Major Deacon and his wife, and Mark Ferrier.'

'Deac and Ferret? Jesus, no. That's not acceptable.'

'What is it, Dad?' Oliver said, coming across to his father, thinking that he had received bad news.

'Nothing. Just a couple of friends of mine can't make it.'

Oliver saw it was nothing important and went back to dancing.

Murdo strode out of the room and nobody gave him a second glance.

He was fuming, just like he always was when he didn't get his own way.

He left, walking into the snow.

'WHAT HAPPENED NEXT?' Dunbar asked as Thomas Deal seemed to have stalled in his story.

He looked at the two detectives. Then seemed to sense he was back in the here and now. 'What? Oh. Yes, well, there was a lull in the music when we all heard the small plane fly overhead. It was so low, I thought it was going to crash into the roof of the hotel.'

'How did you find out it was Murdo flying the plane?'

'We went out, Oliver and I, and saw the car we had come in sitting at the end of the airstrip with its lights on. God knows how he had done it, but he'd got that plane lifted off the airstrip in heavy snow. I didn't even know how the wheels managed to get through, but then somebody told us that Murdo insisted that the airstrip was kept clear of snow all the time. It hadn't long been ploughed.'

'You were sure it was Murdo in the plane?' Harry asked.

'Oh, yes. He asked the control tower over at the airport for permission to take off. It was granted, then off he went. The plane was only on radar for a few minutes before disappearing. It was at first light that they could start a search. Nothing was ever found.'

'Basically, the only one who was at odds with him that night was Oliver, his son?'

'Yes. But if you're thinking he had anything to do with his father's disappearance, then think again. Oliver and I were in a ballroom with more than a hundred other people when the plane went over.'

'Can you tell us who was left what property in Oliver's will?'

'Clive was left the log house, Shona the lodge, and Fenton and Zachary were left a house each. Nothing that will make them rich, but they do share the hotel, the big house. And the business, of course, which *will* make them rich.'

There was a knock on the door and a uniform poked his head round. 'Sorry to disturb you, but we've had a phone call that you should know about.'

Dunbar terminated the interview and let Thomas Deal leave before talking to the uniform.

'We've just found Shona Wolf dead. In her car.'

TWELVE

Debbie Comb and Lillian Young were at the scene of the crash, along with a fire engine and an ambulance. Several patrol cars were in the mix.

The back of the car was draped with a tarpaulin to keep prying eyes away, if there were any, but Harry couldn't see any thrill seekers. Except for a man with a dog who, they had been told, had come across the scene and called it in.

'Hello again,' Debbie said, coming across to the two detectives. 'Nasty one. Her upper torso and head are crushed.'

'She rammed into that JCB?' Harry said. 'How the hell did she manage that?'

'That's what we thought when we turned up, but Lillian came along, simply because of the case with

Shona's brother, Clive, just to have a once-over, and… well, I'll let her explain.'

Both Harry and Dunbar walked past the fire crew and stopped at the front of the car. What was left of the front end had blood spattered on it and they could see a form under a sheet that the fire brigade had put over the victim to stop prying eyes.

'This is not what it seems,' Lillian said.

'What's the problem?' Dunbar said.

'Look into the car from here.' She was standing on the passenger said, so they both went round to look. 'See anything obvious?'

Both men looked in, but nothing jumped out at them.

'Go on then, give us a clue,' Harry said.

'This is a manual gearbox car,' Lillian said. 'It's in reverse. She was trying to reverse the car when the machine hit her. She was trying to get away and it looks like the car stalled. She didn't hit the digger, *it* hit *her*. Somebody drove it into her as she tried to get away.'

Harry took in a deep breath. 'Somebody murdered her.'

'Unless somebody was driving it, and she tried to get the car out of the way, and he didn't see her and hit her, then panicked and ran off.'

'That doesn't even sound right, does it?' Dunbar said.

'Not at all. First of all, the building site is closed down until Monday. Nobody was working here, and we can check with site management, but it doesn't look like there is, or should be, any activity.'

'Somebody was waiting for her,' Harry said. 'Waited until she got in the car and then killed her with the machine.'

'That's what I'm thinking.'

Dunbar nodded to the older man with the dog. 'I think it's unlikely he's the culprit.'

'Agreed. But it's somebody who knows his way around these machines,' Harry said.

'Where's the husband?' Dunbar said. 'What's his name again?'

'Brian Gibbons,' Harry answered.

'Aye. Let's find him and have a word. Meantime, I want to talk to the old bloke with the dog.' Dunbar turned to the pathologist. 'Have you started the post-mortem on Clive Wolf yet?'

'I have. The cause of death was blunt-force trauma to the head.'

'Okay. We'll let you deal with this and talk to you later.'

Dunbar and Harry walked over to where the man with the dog was standing talking to a uniform.

'I'm DCI Dunbar. This is DCI McNeil. We'd like a word.' Dunbar nodded to the uniform to leave, which he did. The dog was medium sized and friendly, just like Dunbar's own dog.

'What's your name, for the record?'

'Arthur Mortimer.'

'Can you tell me what happened, Arthur?' he asked the man.

'I was walking my dog, like I do every day. This is one of our routes. We walk past the fairground, come round the hill and go through the park. Or what used to be a fucking park.'

'I'm sorry?' Harry said.

'This,' Mortimer said, sweeping his free arm around, 'this was just a park at one time; the dog could run about. But some bright spark decided to build houses on it. The land was owned by the Wolf family, and they wanted to be greedy and build houses. There's even going to be a marina over there. God almighty, there will be nothing left soon.'

'Was there anybody about when you got here?' Dunbar asked, looking at the half-finished houses.

'No one. I could faintly hear the music from the festival over there, but there was nothing going on round here. It was all peace and quiet. I thought there had been an accident, so I went over to look. I thought the lassie had run into the digger thing there.'

'How many ways in and out of here?' Harry asked.

'Just the one. The way you came in. The park ends

over there with the trails that lead up into the hills. It's a great walk. You can go up there and come round at the other side. There's a car park down there.'

'You could park round there and walk here over the hill back to your car?' Dunbar asked.

'Aye. That's what me and the wee fella do,' Mortimer said. 'Although my legs are shaking so much, I'm going to walk back round instead of going up the hill. Even if it means going past those freaks again.'

'What freaks?'

'Those carnival freaks. I mean, they've been here for years, but they just look weird. I would never trust them. As soon as I hear my boy here giving it laldy at the front window, I get my cricket bat. One of them will get a fucking smack one day, let me tell you.'

'Have they ever bothered you?' Harry asked.

'Well, no, *they* haven't. But there's always somebody trying to sell religion or something. I mean, not that often on the island, but there're always people coming here from the mainland. I don't trust any of them.'

'How well do you know the Wolf family?'

'I moved here about ten years ago when I retired. My dad used to come here when he was a boy. I fell in love with the place, and the only fly in the ointment is that carnival. As long as they don't bother me, I'll be fine. But the Wolf family do a lot of good here. The only two who live here are Oliver and his son, Clive. *Did*. Since they're both dead. God knows it wouldn't surprise me if they pulled the hotel down and built houses on that land,' Mortimer said.

'You ever see Clive Wolf going about the town?'

'Sure. You know the house he lived in with his father is here on the north island, but he was always out and about on the south island. Especially on a Saturday night, when he would go into some of the bars in town.'

'Did he ever get into trouble?' Dunbar asked.

'He was always mouthing off. Shouting and swearing, getting drunk, then driving home. Nobody really liked him. Up until his father died, he took care of the rental homes here on the island. He was a bad landlord, by all accounts. To be honest, I'm not surprised that somebody lamped him one. I mean, I never had any trouble with him, but I saw it for myself in the pub.'

'Did he bother anybody in particular?'

'I saw him and that big Irish oaf getting into it one night.'

'Irish?' Dunbar said.

'Aye. Big Joe Murphy. He owns the fairground and he's a big lad, but Wolf got in his face. I don't even know what they were arguing about, but Wolf was drunk and he ended up clarting a table over. The polis took him home that night, I think.'

'Was this recently?' Harry asked.

'Naw, it was before his father died. Before last Christmas. Murphy likes a drink, but he's never any bother. He can certainly hold his liquor better than Clive Wolf ever could.'

'Okay, thanks,' Dunbar said. 'If you remember anything else, call the station and they'll get in touch with us.'

'Will do. Can I go now?'

'Yes. But we'd like you to go to the station and make a formal statement about what you saw today.'

The man walked away with his dog.

'We'll need to have a chat with this Irish guy, see what that was all about,' Dunbar said.

'It sounds like Clive Wolf wasn't liked around here.'

'Aye. Maybe he had a lot more enemies than we thought.'

THIRTEEN

He always hated the fairground. Or carnival. Whatever it was called. To him, it was nothing but a bunch of noises and flashing lights. The smell was the worst. It was fine if you were coming here for a night's fun, but when you had to smell it all the time, then it became sickening.

He stepped out from behind two rides and saw the man wandering about. He was supposed to have been in the car, but somehow it was only the woman. Well, he'd have to fix that, wouldn't he? But not before the others. Those wankers were going to get it. This was going to be one weekend they would all remember.

He didn't want to rush things, though. This had to be done carefully. But this was a window of opportunity that he wasn't going to miss. All of them in one place at the same time. It was the golden ticket.

He stood watching the fat bastard walking about. The man was on his phone. No doubt asking somebody to come and pick him up. If he was over here, then it was a safe bet he didn't know yet that his wife was dead. Maybe he was actually calling her, but he would be lucky if he got through to her, not because she was dead but because mobile phone service on this part of the island was patchy at best. Shite at worst.

'What the fuck are you doing standing around here?' he heard a voice say behind him.

It was the old Irish guy, Joe Murphy. Big stature, big mouth. He thought at first the man was talking to him and was about to say something back, but then realised he was talking to the young man standing near him, smoking.

'I'm just waiting to start my shift,' the man said.

'Get a foocking move on, then.' Murphy made it sound like 'forking move on' with his thick accent.

'Yes, sir.'

'Fooking lazy wee bastard.'

The big Irishman walked away and the carny walked away in the opposite direction. Then the Irishman stopped to talk to somebody.

It was Brian Gibbons, the scrounger related to the Wolf family.

He looked Gibbons. Maybe he would deal with this piece of shit after he'd dealt with the others. Just for fun. Why not? It would be just as easy to kill him on the sly and lay him to rest in the sea. In for a penny and all that.

Meantime, he would wander around. Then, tonight, he would go on the hunt.

FOURTEEN

Alex and Evans were in the incident room when Dunbar and Harry got there. It looked like it probably doubled as Santa's grotto at Christmas.

'We've been going through all the information we've got,' Evans said. 'DI Barclay did some digging.'

'As did Ronnie Vallance,' Alex said. 'Since some of them live in Edinburgh.'

'Right,' Harry said. 'Well, Shona Gibbons was murdered.' He went on to explain what they'd discovered.

'Somebody's targeting the Wolf family then,' Alex said.

Harry looked at the whiteboard that she had set up before they got there. 'Let's have a look at them individually.' He took a ruler from a desk and tapped it against one of the photos that had been posted there. Clive Wolf, still sitting in the chair where he had died.

'Give us the rundown on him,' he said to Alex.

'He and Shona were twins. Aged thirty-seven. Shona was on her second marriage, currently to Brian Gibbons. They run their own property development company in Edinburgh. Shona and Clive were born here on the island in the big house. Clive never left. He worked with his father, running the company that had been left to Oliver. Of course, the company wasn't his for seven years, until Murdo was declared dead. No sign of him was ever found, and we now know why: he was sealed up in a wall.'

'Shona left, obviously,' Dunbar said, 'but you said she was married twice. Who was her first husband?'

'He was a financier. He died in a skiing accident fifteen years ago. They'd only been married two years at the time.'

'Has anybody spoken to Gibbons yet?' Harry said.

'He got out of a taxi when we were just leaving. We took him inside and told him. When I asked him where he had been, he said he had walked to the fairground and spoke to an Irishman, Joe Murphy, who he knows.'

'We'll check that out later.'

'What about Clive?' Dunbar asked.

'He liked the women,' Evans answered. 'He was

never short of a girlfriend, but he never married. He lived in the big house with his father, and Oliver died there last Christmas. Two days before Christmas.'

'And nobody thought of questioning the coincidence?'

'Apparently not, sir.'

'What about that other pair of loud mouths?'

'Zachary Wolf is in finance. He lives and works in Glasgow Divorced.'

'Where was he born?' Harry asked.

'They were all born here on the island, sir. They all moved away in adulthood.'

'Where's their mother?'

'She died years ago,' Alex answered.

'What about the family mouthpiece?' Dunbar said.

'Fenton Wolf is a doctor. A cardiologist. Works in Glasgow. Also divorced.'

'What was Oliver Wolf's cause of death?'

'Cardiac arrest.'

Dunbar looked at him for a moment. 'A bit ironic, isn't it? The son is a cardiologist and his father dies of a heart attack. Anybody else feel the hairs on their neck going up?'

'You think he might have been murdered too?' Harry asked.

'I'm not discounting it. Two of the Wolf family are

dead. Seven months after their old man died. You know how suspicious we get, Harry.'

'We can ask around and see if we can get hold of the death certificate. If not, we can have it pulled. Did he die here on the island?'

Alex nodded. 'At home.'

'Somebody knew where old Murdo Wolf was and for some reason they were trying to get him out of that wall. To move him? Probably. But why? It has to be connected to the memorial for Oliver Wolf and the fact that the kids were being given the properties.' Dunbar looked at Alex. 'Did you find out what else they own here?'

'Some of the land on the north island. Obviously their house and the hotel next to it, but they also owned the park where the new houses are being built. Where they found Shona. And they own the land where the carnival sits. And they once owned the hotel where we're staying, the Laoch Lodge. But after Murdo was declared dead, it was given to the Shaw family. Murdo left it to Shaw in his will.'

'Crail Shaw, the man who was his driver and assistant?' Dunbar said.

'Yes. Murdo must have thought a lot of him,' Harry said.

'We need to find out who benefits from these

deaths. Like, do the remaining brothers benefit from the twins' deaths?'

'I think it goes deeper than that, Jimmy.' Harry looked at the board. 'I mean, they're not stupid people, so killing their siblings in the hope of getting the property left to them would be dumb.'

'We've both seen dumber criminals, neighbour.'

'True. But these laddies are professional people. They're not stupid.' Harry was silent for a moment. Then: 'One of you find out if Oliver Wolf was buried or cremated.'

'I already know the answer,' Evans said. 'He was buried. He's in the island's only cemetery.'

'It might be worth having him exhumed,' Alex said.

'That's something we can consider if we have to. Meantime, we have to go and have a talk with a man called Joe Murphy.'

Dunbar looked at his watch. 'We should get something to eat before places start to fill up. We don't know if those reprobates from the music festival will come down here and take up all the tables.'

'They usually just drink lager and eat crisps for dinner,' Harry said. 'Just ask Alex. She's the expert on living in a tent.'

'Once,' Alex said, holding a finger up. 'One time I went to T in the Park.'

'Willingly?' Dunbar asked. 'My laddie went there

one time and had to burn his jeans when he came back home. I didn't even want to ask.'

'How about you, Robbie?' Harry asked.

'Not my scene, sir. I prefer sports myself.'

'I can confirm that,' Dunbar said. 'In fact, he's expecting Andy Murray round tonight for a wee game of...something.'

Harry and Alex waited for more but nothing came.

'Anyway, how about it?' Dunbar said. 'Hit a wee place just now, then we can talk to this guy Murphy. And we still have to talk to the Wolf brothers. And we have to find Brian Gibbons and break the news about the death of his wife.'

'And ask him where he was at the time,' Harry added.

They left the station and found a little restaurant in the main street. 'Tuck in, people. This is on Police Scotland,' Dunbar said.

FIFTEEN

He stood looking down at his father's grave. The sun was still out but a wind had got up, whipping through the trees that provided shade in the small cemetery. Mount Beacon poked its head up above the treeline, like it was being nosy.

He heard a twig snap in the long grass.

'You're late,' he said to his brother.

'I was making sure people saw me.'

'Is it done?'

'It is. There's just one problem.'

He turned to his brother. 'I don't like problems, you know that.'

'Problems are just roadblocks. We just work our way around them. We meet the challenge head on and deal with it.'

'It's a pity about that fucker McInsh and his dog.'

'Let's not do anything silly. McInsh would hand you your arse on a plate. I can take of the others, but I'm not going to put myself at risk. There can't be any collateral damage. This is going to be bad enough without any extras added into the mix.'

'I understand that. It's just a pity we couldn't rope him into this.'

'It would have been easier if he didn't have an alibi,' his brother said.

'That would have taken a lot longer to plan, and time was against us.' He turned to look back at his father's grave. 'But let's focus on the job at hand. We have this weekend and that's it. We're not going to get a better opportunity, so let's stick to the plan.'

'Agreed. Those officers from the mainland could be a problem.'

'No, they won't be. It's something we planned for. Do you think they would let that daft bastard Turnbull investigate? He couldn't investigate the froth on the top of his pint. No, it was always going to be a detective in a murder case. We just need to keep putting them off the scent.'

'Easier said than done.'

'No, it's not. We've gone over everything. Just stay level-headed and this will be over before we know it.'

His brother smiled. 'I'm more than happy to take out that copper if he gets in my way.'

He looked at him. 'Which one?'

'Any of them. All of them. I don't care.'

He put a hand on his brother's shoulder. 'Just listen to your older brother and we'll be fine.'

SIXTEEN

The carnival's owners were hoping that the music festival would have a knock-on effect on their takings, and they were mostly right.

'Ever been to a concert, neighbour?' Dunbar asked.

'Aye. We went to see Genesis in London, two thousand and seven. We went away for a long weekend. It was great.'

'What about you, Alex?' Evans said.

'I hate to admit it, but I've only been to T in the Park. I've never been to a concert to see one group. What about you?'

'Nothing that he would admit to,' Dunbar said. 'He does like Wimbledon, though.'

'Anyway, what's the difference between a carnival and a fairground?' Evans asked, eager to change the subject.

'I think a carnival is like a circus; it travels around. But a fairground is like the Pleasure Beach in Blackpool,' Harry said. 'This one here, the carnival joins on to the fairground for the summer.'

'How do you know so much about it?' Alex asked him.

'I read a pamphlet in the hotel. And guess where Old Man Boxer gets his name from?' Harry replied, nodding to a painted board outside a tent.

'Christ, he's a carny boxer,' Dunbar said. 'You can pay to fight him.' He looked at Evans. 'Now's your chance to give him a good skelp.'

'Really? I don't want to hurt the old bloke.'

A young man walked out, holding paper towels to his face. The blood had been roughly cleaned up from his face and a friend was supporting him while holding on to his shirt.

'You could always go, sir,' Evans said. 'I mean, I would put money on you winning, of course.'

'Why would I want to fight cleanly?'

'Roll up! Roll up! Challenge the boxer to a fight!' a young man shouted through a megaphone. He was dressed like a ringmaster. 'Go five rounds, win a hundred pounds!'

Harry locked eyes with him; it was Brendan Shaw.

'You, sir!' the young man shouted. 'Come inside.

You look like a hard man. Beat the boxer, win some cash.'

'Go on, Harry,' Alex said.

'Decorum, wife of mine. A senior officer can't be seen to participate in such frivolous activity when he's on duty.'

She sighed. 'Oh well, I can only try.'

'You don't need a hundred pounds that desperately.'

'I don't mean me fight him. Anyway, it's not about the money. It's showing that old fool that he can't talk to anybody any way he likes.'

'He must be fit, though, neighbour,' Dunbar said. 'Nothing a good kick in the bollocks wouldn't take care of, but that's not in the Queensberry rules.'

'I wouldn't go in there with him,' they heard a voice say from behind them. 'He has weighted gloves.'

Nancy Shaw, the owner of the Laoch Lodge and Boxer's wife, was standing watching the ringmaster touting for business.

'I didn't know your son was part of this business,' Harry said.

'That's Jack, Brendan's twin brother. Brendan doesn't get involved. Jack, on the other hand, laps all of this up.'

'Your husband been doing this for a long time?' Dunbar asked.

'For more years than I can remember.' She had a light jacket on and pulled it around herself more as a cool wind came in off the sea. She looked from her son to Dunbar. 'He didn't always need the weights in his gloves. But the years and the drink got hold of him.'

'Does Jack box as well?' Alex asked.

'Oh, no, love. Jack is good at talking but not at fighting. A wet paper bag would make a fool of him. But he has the gift of the gab, as you can see.'

'Did you hear about Shona Wolf?' Dunbar asked.

'I did. You can't sneeze on the island without somebody knowing about it. But that sort of thing could happen to anybody. Accidents happen every day.'

Dunbar looked at Harry for a moment, before looking back at Nancy. 'She was murdered, Mrs Shaw. Word is going to get out anyway.'

'I heard it was an accident. Good God, that's awful.'

'When you're a powerful family like the Wolf family, you make enemies,' Harry said.

Nancy turned towards him. 'I'm sure that's true in every business, but they did so much for this island. They brought it to life. I have never heard a bad word said against them.'

'Except by somebody called Joe Murphy,' Dunbar said. 'You know him?'

'Joe? Yes. He runs the carnival. He comes here

every year. He's a big Irishman with a big temper. He likes a drink, naturally.'

'You know where we can get hold of him?'

'I'm not sure, but he's always around. He runs a tight ship. Nobody messes with Joe. Has he done anything wrong?'

'That's what we want to establish. He was seen arguing in the pub with Clive Wolf recently.'

'Clive was just like Joe – hot-headed. I did hear about that, but it sounded like something over nothing.'

'What does he look like?' Harry asked.

Nancy was about to say something when she nodded. 'That's Joe over there.'

The four detectives turned in the direction she was looking. A big man dressed in a checked shirt and jeans looked back at them.

They walked over to him. He stood a good four inches taller than Harry.

'We're with Police Scotland, MIT,' Harry said.

'Aye, I know who you fooking are. The whole island knows who you fooking are,' Joe Murphy said.

'Bad for business, are we?' Dunbar said.

'People get nervous when youse bastards are around. Even when they've done fook all.'

'If you've done nothing, then there's fuck all to be nervous about, is there? But we want to ask you about the night you had an argument with Clive Wolf in the pub.'

Joe Murphy laughed, his big head tilting back. 'I wondered when the fook you would be round here busting me fooking balls about that. Well, let me tell you something, laddie.' He poked a finger towards Dunbar's chest and Evans stepped forward. Joe Murphy turned his attention to him. 'You his wee terrier, son?'

'The name's DS Robbie Evans. Just so you won't ever forget me.'

'Is that right?' Murphy laughed again. 'Just like that wee fooking shite Clive Wolf thought he was a wee hard man. Back where I come from, we eat wee fookers like him for breakfast.' He tried poking Evans in the chest, but Evans saw the move coming a mile off and grabbed the big, meaty appendage and twisted it, bending it back.

Murphy's eyes went wide and he let out a screech.

Evans leant in close. 'Back where I come from, your fucking face would be broken by now. Police Scotland might frown upon me smacking an old fucker like you, but they most certainly won't frown upon me defending myself and just happening to break your finger into the bargain. In front of senior officers no less. So, if you want to carry on your shite, just try to fucking poke me again. Understand?'

The big Irishman was almost on his knees, almost looking like he was having a heart attack. Some people were looking at the tableau playing out before them but most couldn't care less. It was almost as if this was a sideshow.

'Yes!' Murphy hissed through clenched teeth.

Evans let his finger go and the Irishman stood up. Harry thought for a moment he was going to go for it, but after spending years reading people's body language, he knew Evans would have decked Murphy.

'There, now that we've got that settled, neighbour,' Dunbar said, 'maybe you would like to give us your side of the story about the night you had a run-in with Clive Wolf, before we get a platoon of uniforms over from the mainland with a search warrant and we close this funland down for a week while we search it.'

Murphy was flushed and rubbing his finger. They suspected that if it had been anybody else who had bent his finger, there might have been more words said, but the prospect of losing a fortune if the carnival was shut down made him bite his tongue.

'Clive Wolf was a regular in the Sunset Arms. It's one of the better boozers on the island, where locals go to drink. I mean, it's not the sort of place where you get rolled in the toilets of course, not like some of the shite I've been inside in Glasgow, but it's where you can go and have a drink without being bothered by the tourists. There're plenty of bars on the island where they can go, like the theme bars. Those shitey Irish places that are about as authentic as a three-pound coin. But anyway, Clive liked to frequent the Sunset Arms as well, and he was a pain in the arse when he got drunk.'

'Who started the argument?' Alex asked.

Murphy turned to her. 'He did. Plenty of witnesses will tell you. Clive was an obnoxious wee bastard at times, and for some reason he was even more obnoxious that night. He hadn't been right ever since his father died. It hit him hard, so people cut him some slack. But that night, I'd had too much to drink and he rubbed me the wrong way.'

'Where we come from, that's almost as good as a confession,' Dunbar said.

'Look, I didn't kill the wee bastard. I never touched him. Yes, we had words, but it never got physical. I would have broken his fooking neck, but he wasn't worth wasting my time on.'

'Did you know where he lived?'

'Of course I do. Everybody does. But I wouldn't dirty me hands. I heard he was found in the old loch house.'

'He was. Ever been there?' Dunbar said.

'No. Never set foot in the place.'

'I'll have an officer take your prints down at the station, just so we have a comparison.'

'You what? That's against me civil liberties.'

'You want ruled out or not? Or do you still want us on your back?' Harry said.

'Fine. I'll go down to the station tomorrow. But you're wasting your time. I never touched Clive Wolf.'

'Do you know Brian Gibbons?' Dunbar asked.

'I know him, yes. Why?'

'He said he was talking to you this afternoon. Do you remember that?'

'Of course I do. Do you think I'm daft?'

'What time?'

'How would I know? Early afternoon or something.'

The big man turned and walked away without looking back.

'What do you think?' Harry said.

'I think he's all piss and wind,' Dunbar said. 'I'm sure the bit about the argument was right, but they're still lifting prints and when he gives us his, we'll find out if he was telling the truth about being in there.'

He spotted somebody further ahead. 'Muckle!' he shouted.

McInsh was with his dog and a woman who was walking a Beagle on a leash.

'Jimmy! This is my wife, Wilma. With Nessie.'

The woman smiled at them. 'How do.'

Dunbar introduced them all before turning to Muckle. 'Listen, son, I wanted a word if you don't mind.'

'Sure.' Muckle turned to Wilma. 'Be back in a sec, love.' He walked away with Sparky and Dunbar.

'You know I can't ask you to go and look at those houses, but did you write down the addresses?'

'I did.' Muckle reached into a pocket and brought out a piece of paper. 'Wouldn't it be easier if I just showed you? I mean, I don't have to go in. I could just bring the dog and wait outside.'

'Aye, why don't we do that. Where's your pal tonight?'

'He's away off somewhere with his boyfriend.'

'Have you decided what you're going to do about a job?'

'Nah. Not yet. I'll leave the island, though. I've already told Wilma, and she's quite happy for us to go back to the mainland. I've been giving some thought to starting up a wee investigation business on the mainland. Maybe Wee Shug will join me.'

'You could always join the force again,' Dunbar said.

'Thanks, sir, but there are a lot of bastards still in uniform who shouldn't be.'

'We're trying to weed them out. You and Shug

would be fine. You could always work Govan again. My team are brand new.'

'I'll keep it in mind. First, though, let's go and have a look at those places.'

They walked back to the group.

Harry was looking at the fairground rides. A rollercoaster, the waltzers, a ghost train ride. And all the little stalls in between. Coloured lights flashed more prominently in the descending darkness. Music filled the air, not just from the concert down the road, but the familiar chintzy music played in fairgrounds the world over.

He could hear a bingo caller shouting out the numbers. Carnies were encouraging the public to spend a fortune on a stuffed gonk. Throw a wonky dart at a playing card tacked to the wall. Knock metal cans down.

'Brings back memories, eh?' Alex said.

Harry didn't hear her for a moment. 'What? Oh, yeah. Good times. Chance had a great time at Burntisland. We could never get him off the wee fire engine that went round on a track with some other cars.'

'Hopefully we can make some good memories too, with our own kids.'

He smiled and put a hand on hers. 'We will. I promise.'

Dunbar walked back over. 'I just had a call from

Thomas Deal, the solicitor. He wants us to head over to the house. The boys have turned back up. With Brian Gibbons. There's a ruckus going on.'

'Let's go.'

'You want me to come up?' Muckle asked.

'Best not, my friend. Things could go south for you now that you're not in an official capacity.'

'You've got my number. Give me a shout if you need me. That Sergeant Turnbull is about as much use as an ashtray on a motorbike.'

SEVENTEEN

Whatever had gone down in the house was now over.

'I tried to tell them,' Thomas Deal said. He was standing in front of the fire with a glass in his hand. 'But what do I know?'

'He started it!' Brian Gibbons said, pointing to Fenton. 'And I finished it.'

'Finished what? Fucking twat,' Fenton answered.

'Let's get you cleaned up,' Missy Galbraith said. The solicitor's assistant was fussing around like a mother hen. She was younger than any of them but acted twice her age. She handed Brian a damp cloth, then left the room.

'Leave me alone,' Brian said, holding a bloodied hanky to his nose.

'Were you with Shona today before she died?' Dunbar said to him.

'I just went for a walk after she stormed off,' Brian answered.

Fenton looked at him like he had two heads. 'What did you say?'

Zach, who had been sitting in an armchair, jumped up. 'Our sister's dead?'

'You haven't heard?' Harry said. 'It's all over the island. People start talking before we have a chance to talk to the family.'

'Heard what? I didn't hear anything.' Fenton said. 'Did he know?' He pointed to Gibbons.

'I'm sorry to say, we're treating her death as suspicious,' Dunbar said, ignoring the question.

'What does that mean?' Fenton asked.

'It means we don't think she died of natural causes.' Harry explained where Shona had been found but not the exact circumstances.

'Fucking murdered?' Fenton looked at Brian. 'Oh, you old, fat bastard. I knew my sister shouldn't have married you.' He took two steps towards the older man.

'That's enough!' Dunbar said. 'We need to talk to you all. Not Mr Deal, but you two, Fenton and Zachary. I want to know where you were today. You too, Mr Gibbons. I want to know exactly where you were before you went to the fairground.'

Fenton curled his lip. 'Where were we? We were looking around at the houses our father left to us.

Nothing more, nothing less. We had dinner in a little restaurant on the south island. Here,' he said, fishing his wallet out of a pocket. He opened it up and took out a receipt. 'You never know when somebody will screw you over, so I always keep the receipts until the credit card bill comes in.'

He passed it over and Dunbar looked at it. It was marked for a couple of hours previously.

'What about you, Mr Gibbons?' Dunbar said, handing the receipt back. 'Where were you?'

'I left Shona on the hill overlooking the fairground. Well, the new houses on the other side. I walked over to the fairground. The mobile phone reception is better there. I called for a taxi. I spoke to Joe Murphy like I already said, and then I came home. Where the two young detectives were waiting.'

'The houses that you and my father are building,' Zach said. 'If you want to know who had a motive, it's him! With Shona out of the way, the business is all his and he'll get her money.'

Harry looked at the old solicitor. 'Is that true? Did Shona leave a will?'

'Even if she didn't, he'd be entitled to it. But yes, they both have reciprocating wills. Brian will indeed inherit everything that was Shona's, including her share of the hotel and the business.' Deal drank some of the Scotch from the glass in his hand.

'Dirty bastard,' Fenton said.

'Fenton!' Deal said. 'I have worked for your father and your family for a very long time. Long before you were born. I can assure you that nothing underhanded has ever been done. Every business deal your father made, every one that your grandfather made, was above board. I know for a fact that the housing deal he went into with Brian was legitimate. Shona knew of it, you and your brother knew of it. So why the accusations now?'

Harry was impressed by the old man's outburst, silencing the two brothers.

'I know, you're right,' Fenton said, 'but this has got everybody shaken. Who would want to murder our brother and sister?'

'Either somebody has a grudge or they stand to gain from it,' Alex said. 'If we can find somebody with either motive, then we can find our killer.'

'Look, I know it doesn't look good,' Zach said, 'us being out and about, but we're not going to get anywhere turning on each other.'

'That's easy for you to say,' Brian said, dabbing at his lip again. Missy came back in with another cloth.

'This one has ice in it,' she said, giving him the new one.

He crumpled the bloody tissue and put it in a pocket. 'Thank you.'

'The memorial is going ahead tomorrow?' Dunbar said.

'It is,' Fenton said. 'People are already here. They want to pay their last respects to my father. And now my brother and sister.'

'The hotel *is* busy with his friends,' said Deal. 'I was talking with a few earlier, people I have known for many years. They said they were shocked to learn of Clive's death, but they want to say a proper goodbye to Oliver. The ballroom is already set up.'

'I suppose, under the circumstances, there's no reason to postpone it. But I have to ask you not to leave the island,' Harry said, looking at each member of the family in turn.

'We hadn't planned on leaving for another week,' Fenton said. 'We just wanted to see our houses, then make plans to rent them out. I don't think any of us had planned to sell. Even Shona.' He threw a look at Brian, but the older man was in too much pain with his rapidly swelling lip to give a comeback.

'You know, son,' Dunbar said, 'for a doctor, you're pretty aggressive.'

'In my game, you have to be. I'm not aggressive to my patients.'

'I should damn well hope not.' Dunbar looked at Brian. 'We'll talk to Brendan. See if he remembers talking to you.'

'Do that.'

'However, if the fairground is on the other side of the hill,' Harry said, 'you could have killed Shona and then walked over.'

'I swear to God I didn't kill her.'

'Don't leave town, Mr Gibbons,' Harry said. 'We'll talk again in the morning.'

EIGHTEEN

Brendan Shaw was doing his stint as barman behind the Laoch Lodge's bar.

'Lounge bar at night, breakfast bar in the morning,' he said with a smile. 'What can I get you folks?'

Harry ordered a pint for himself and a Diet Coke for Alex. Evans had a lager and Dunbar had the same.

'Put your money away, folks,' Brendan said. 'My mum says to look after you.'

'Nonsense, son,' Dunbar said, loosening his tie. 'This is on Police Scotland. And you have a business to run. It's not a charity you run.'

'Unlike the Wolf family, eh?' Brendan said, pouring the drinks.

'What do you mean?' Harry asked as Alex and Evans got a table.

'Oh, nothing. I mean, Murdo Wolf made so much

money, he created a foundation. He was a great philanthropist. So was Oliver. He strived to make the island the best it could ever be. No properties were ever run down or left in a state of disrepair. The hospital has the latest equipment and the schools are top class, even though we don't have a ton of schoolkids. The ones we do have get the best education, with every one of them getting a scholarship to get a degree on the mainland. Aye, the Wolf family are tops.'

He handed over the pints and the Coke.

'We saw your brother down at the fairground with your dad,' Dunbar said.

'Two peas in a pod, we are,' Brendan said, grinning. 'But I prefer to keep a bit more low key. Jack's the showman. He loves enticing men to fight my dad. None of them have ever won, but I told Dad, one day some young Turk will come up there and knock your socks off. I wish he would retire, but he's stubborn.'

'It comes to us eventually,' Dunbar said, waving Evans back over. 'Grab a pint, son.' Then he turned back to Brendan. 'Do you remember talking to Brian Gibbons at the fairground this afternoon?'

'Aye. I saw him there. I was having a wee wander around and bumped into him.'

'When was this?'

'Oh, early afternoon sometime. I don't know the exact time.'

'Okay, thanks.'

Evans took two pints back to the table as Harry carried his and Alex's drink over. Dunbar said he never had two full hands when he was in a pub, in case he had to use one of them quickly. Harry said he would be more than happy to head-butt somebody if his hands were full.

'I don't think we'll be having any problems in here,' he added, looking around at the clientele. A couple who looked to be in their fifties, clearly American. Harry couldn't tell if the biggest giveaway was the accents or the husband's Hawaiian shirt. A young couple who were on holiday and a few of the other guests. Nothing that would cause Brendan to break into a sweat.

'You know, I would have Brian Gibbons sweating in an interview room on suspicion of killing his wife if I actually thought he was capable of doing it,' Dunbar said.

'Agreed. Fenton said Shona wanted to talk to Gibbons out in the open and one of her favourite places was the trail that leads over the hill. I think Shona Wolf would have booted his nuts for him.'

'And it's not like he's fit enough to walk up the hill, go back down to kill his wife, then walk over the hill to the fairground,' Evans said. 'Unless they didn't actually make it up the hill, but that wouldn't fit in with the scenario.'

'Explain,' Dunbar said, taking a drink.

'We know she was feisty and didn't take any guff off her husband, who is twenty years older than her, so late fifties. She's fitter. Let's say they park up. Gibbons knows he's got to get into the JCB and reverse it into the car. You think Shona Wolf would sit there and watch her husband climb into that thing? Personally, I think she would be jumping out asking him what the hell he was doing.'

'I agree,' Alex said. 'To kill Clive Wolf first, then his wife? Besides, he has an alibi for the time of Clive's death.'

'That doesn't mean he didn't kill his wife,' Harry said.

'Brian Gibbons has one foot in the grave if he doesn't do something about losing weight. I don't see him being fit enough to kill his wife.'

'She's got a point, neighbour,' said Dunbar. 'There's another reason behind the killing, and it's not Brian Gibbons' building plans.'

'We need to ask Thomas Deal what would happen if they all died. All the beneficiaries,' Harry said. 'Who would benefit if they were all out of the picture. Including Brian Gibbons.'

'Maybe the foundation that Brendan there was talking about,' said xxx.

'Maybe,' said Dunbar. 'We'll find out tomorrow. Meantime, let's have another drink, then I'm away to FaceTime the wife.'

They went upstairs. Alex was in the shower and Harry was settling down to watch some TV when his mobile phone told him there was a text message.

He took it out and read it.

Can you meet me? You told me to contact you if I wanted to.

It was from a number he didn't recognise but the initial was *M*.

He typed back, *Who am I talking to?*

Alex came out of the en suite, drying her hair. 'Talking to another woman while I'm in the shower,' she said, joking.

'I think I am,' he replied. She frowned and sat down on the bed beside him. He showed her the message just as the answer to his question popped onto the screen.

Missy.

NINETEEN

Harry could hear the waves crashing on the shore in the distance as he stood with his collar up. He could sense the sea and smell it, but darkness hid the water.

In the distance, he could hear the fairground in full swing, its day dying slowly until all the last customers were gone. The last gig at the music festival was over; the island's council had stipulated that it must come to a close before the fairground and carnival.

The house he was outside was in total darkness. The north island. The very tip, where people came to walk the trails and spot birds and whatever else outdoorsy people liked doing on an island whose neighbour was New York City thousands of miles to the east.

He hadn't taken the car right up to the house. He

might not be a rocket scientist, but he was a damn good copper and he knew full well that this could be a trap.

He had parked the car at a hikers' car park and walked up a trail, his eyes adjusting to the gloom. He wondered if it had been a deliberate act, back in the day, to keep all the businesses on the south island and keep the north island for accommodation. And the fairground.

Whatever it was, it had worked. This house had an unobstructed view to the Statue of Liberty. If your eyes were that good and your vision could bend over the horizon. The imagination could provide the sight if the ocular abilities weren't quite up to snuff.

He felt the cold and was glad he had worn his jacket and woollen hat. That was one thing with a Scottish summer: pack for every season. A wind whipped through the trees surrounding the property, and he was well-hidden by a large one. The headlight beams from the car announced its arrival, the driver foregoing a stealthy approach. It was a BMW 5 Series, dark in colour with superb lights cutting through the darkness, illuminating the driveway. He ducked behind the tree, but there was little chance he would be spotted in the dark.

He waited until he heard the beep of the remote button locking the car before looking round again.

The driver walked up the steps of the house and

onto the porch. It was a stone and log affair, but nothing like he would have expected to see in Scotland. If he didn't know better, he would have thought he'd been transported to the Canadian Rockies.

A light came on above the front door as the driver went in. Harry moved as silently as he could to the back of the house, away from the car, which sat empty now, waiting to steal its occupant away.

Watching where he put his feet, he rolled the woollen hat down until it morphed into a ski mask. The idea was to keep himself from being seen, not to scare the living daylights out of somebody. When he saw it was all clear, he would present himself at the front door.

He looked through a window into what turned out to be a kitchen. The back garden backed onto the woods, offering plenty of privacy. A few kitchen cabinet lights had been turned on, but there was no sign of the driver of the car.

There was also no sign of anybody else in the house.

He ducked and made his way round to the front of the house, ducking below the living room window. He stood up at the front door and was putting an ear to it when suddenly the door swung open.

He drew a fist back, but stopped when he saw there was no threat. He pulled the ski mask off.

'I thought you were never going to get round to coming to the front door,' Missy Galbraith said.

'I was just making sure it was you.'

'Don't stand there; come in and I'll make coffee.'

He walked in, fairly sure he wasn't going to be ambushed, but the copper in him inspected every element of the hallway. Sensing no threat, he followed her through to the kitchen he had just seen through the window minutes earlier.

'Nice place,' he said.

'It's Zachary Wolf's now. If he lives long enough to claim it. Milk and sugar?'

'Milk, please. What do you mean, "if he lives long enough"? Are you just going by recent events or do you know something? The reason you asked me along here?'

'A little of both,' Missy said, pouring boiling water into two mugs. She stirred in the instant granules and added milk from the fridge. 'Come on, let's take these through to the living room.'

Harry hadn't paid too much attention to Missy's facial features, but up close she appeared to be a little older than he'd first thought. They each sat on a large, comfortable chair with a side table.

'What is this place?' he asked, taking a sip of the coffee. He was tired now, the combination of the long day, the flight and something that Edinburgh didn't have an abundance of these days: fresh air.

'It's the house that Clive Wolf was left in the will.'

'Does this have any bearing on his murder?' Harry said.

'I think it does.'

'That's why you sent me a text asking me to meet you here?'

She drank some of her coffee. 'Yes. Clive was scared. He confided in me. People thought he was just some stuck-up spoiled brat, but I saw a different side to him. I would come across here with Thomas when Oliver needed some legal work done. I've been with the firm for five years now and I've got to know the Wolf family very well. But there's been a shift in the whole dynamic of the Wolf clan.'

'What do you mean?'

'There's just something not quite right about the heirs. Of course, they used to squabble at family gatherings, but not all the time. And now there's an air of fear, for want of a better word. That's why Clive came to me and confided in me.'

'What about?' Harry loosened his jacket. The logs in the fire were crackling and spitting but the heat they kicked out felt good.

'He was scared, Harry. Scared for his life. The only other person he trusted in the world was his twin sister,

Shona. But he knew I could keep a confidence. Thomas and I came across from the mainland a few days ago, to prepare for the memorial and get things up and running. Shortly afterwards, Clive met me here, in private.' She paused for a moment. Drank some of her coffee.

'He overheard people talking, in the big house. He couldn't make out everything that was being said. But one thing he did hear was them talking about where Murdo Wolf was buried.'

'Why didn't he contact us?'

Missy looked at him for a moment. 'Who would have believed him? Clive had been known to shout his mouth off. Not many people liked him, especially Sergeant Turnbull. So Clive did the next best thing: he went looking himself.'

'It's just as well you weren't with him, or else you might have been a victim too.'

'Trust me, I wanted to go with him last night. He wouldn't hear of it. He asked me to stay and be his eyes and ears in the house.'

Harry drank more coffee, feeling the effects of the heat from the fire starting to grip him. The warmth was nice. Summer was never roasting in Scotland, but being on an island that was wide open to the Atlantic didn't help. The last thing he wanted was to doze off.

'Did you hear anything?' he asked.

'No, nothing. They were all about how they were going to spend their money.'

'Let me ask you what you think of them.'

'They were typical spoilt brats. I know people thought Clive was spoilt, but whenever he was across on the mainland we had dinner and he was really good fun. He treated me like a lady. Unlike some of the animals I've been out with.'

'He trusted you, in other words.'

She looked at the floor for a moment before answering. 'Yes, he trusted me completely. And I trusted him. He was the only Wolf family member I would trust.'

'Do you think one of them killed him?'

'I wouldn't put it past them. But all I know is, he left that afternoon and I didn't see him again. I couldn't go looking for him, because that would have shown my hand. But the others were in the hotel, helping out with the memorial. Whoever killed him, I don't think it was one of the Wolf clan.'

'Did he give you any sort of idea who he overheard talking about killing old Murdo?'

Missy looked at the fire before looking back at Harry. 'I wish I had pressed him more to remember, but all he said was that it was two men.'

'We know it wasn't Fenton and Zach, because they were only children at the time.'

POINT OF NO RETURN

'If Clive knew, he didn't say.'

They both heard the creak of the floorboards at the same time. Just before all the lights in the house went out.

The interior door banged open and a masked figure ran in, illuminated only by the flickering light from the fire.

Harry saw the man was holding a hammer. He dropped his cup, reached over for a burning log, grabbed hold of it and swiped it at the running man. This stopped the attacker in his tracks.

Missy threw herself sideways off the chair and rolled behind Harry. She too grabbed a burning log as Harry advanced on the attacker, who was now swinging the hammer ferociously. Harry was well aware that it would only take one hit from the tool to disable or possibly kill him.

Still he advanced on the man, gaining ground, until they heard glass smashing from the kitchen at the back of the house. Then the sound of an explosion, like a petrol bomb had just gone off.

Harry took his eye off the ball for a second and the attacker lunged, but Missy got a strike in, hitting his arm and setting fire to his jacket. It caught and went up. He unzipped it, not taking his eyes off Harry, and threw the burning apparel towards the curtains, where the licking flames caught and spread.

They couldn't see his face because of the mask, not unlike the one Harry had been wearing when he approached. More glass breaking, more flames and they were spreading closer. Thick smoke was creeping into the living room as the attacker turned and fled.

Harry and Missy were about to run outside, but the flames took hold of the back of the house. The fire exploded all around them.

Then Missy was on her feet, pulling on Harry's arm as he struggled to get up. He was standing again, but the way out was on fire.

'This way!' Missy shouted, pulling him through a doorway on one side of the living room. They ran along a short corridor and Missy pushed a door that was ajar. It led into a bedroom. She ran over to a window and opened it, and they climbed out into the fresh air.

Harry started coughing and put a hand over his mouth.

'We can't stay here or we'll be trapped!' Missy shouted. They could both see the house was well alight now, the fire spreading like a disease.

They ran round the side of the house and came to the parking area. The BMW had been given the same treatment as the house. They could hear a car's engine roaring as it hit the road further down.

Harry took his phone out and dialled treble nine.

He hung up and called Jimmy Dunbar, not wanting to panic Alex.

Then he looked at Missy. 'Two men. One with a hammer, trying to kill us. The same people who killed Clive.' Then he hung up.

'We don't know the second person is a man,' she answered. 'It probably is, but you, being a copper, should know better than to jump to conclusions.'

'Point taken.'

Then all they could do was stand and watch the house burn.

TWENTY

Harry didn't know if he was shaking more because of the come-down from the adrenaline rush or the rollicking Alex was giving him.

'Jesus. Don't you ever do that to me again, Harry McNeil,' she said.

'Changed days when a junior officer talks to her DCI like that,' Missy said in a whisper as they stood at the back of the ambulance.

'She's also my wife,' he said as Alex was looking over to the fire service fighting the fire.

'Oh. Then she has every right. If I were your wife, I would be giving you a ticking-off too.'

He raised an eyebrow. 'You invited me here, remember?'

'I'm not your wife.'

'Women stick together; that's the problem.'

'We also have good hearing,' Alex said, turning back to him. 'We're also allowed to vent. Isn't that right, Missy?'

'She's got you bang to rights there, Harry. But to be fair, I did ask him along here. I thought we'd be safe. Nobody knew I was coming here.'

'What about your boss, Deal?'

'He was already in bed. I didn't tell anybody, and as far as I knew, I wasn't followed. I mean, I'm not a secret agent, but it would have been easy to tell if there had been another pair of headlights following me.'

'Somebody knew you were here, or coming here,' Harry said. 'But unless you told them, they didn't know I would be here.'

'It seems like taking a sledgehammer to crack a nut,' Dunbar said. 'It was a bit extreme, using firebombs like that.'

'You think it might have been the Wolf boys?' Evans said. 'I mean, you said it was two men.'

'The thing is, why would they destroy this house? If they're wanting money, then they just saw a lot of it go up in a pile of smoke,' Harry said.

'Could be just a cover,' Dunbar said. 'Wanting to put us off the trail.'

'Whoever it was, they're out to cause mayhem.'

They turned as a patrol car came rushing into the parking area in front of the house, which was no mean feat considering it was already tight with vehicles, including the shell of the BMW, which was now a metal hulk.

Sergeant Turnbull jumped out of the passenger seat, leaving a constable sitting behind the wheel.

'Where's the car we were using?' Dunbar asked.

'It's been wrecked, sir. Windows smashed, tyres slashed. It won't be going anywhere except on the back of a tow truck.'

'Looks like you could have been followed, squire,' Dunbar said to Harry.

'I didn't see them.'

'Maybe they knew where you were going in advance.'

'How, though?' Harry said.

Alex looked at Missy. 'Thomas Deal knew you were coming here?'

'No. I didn't tell anybody. I just slipped out.'

'Where were Fenton and Zach?'

Missy shrugged. 'Your guess is as good as mine. I haven't seen them. They're acting very strange.'

'I don't think you should be staying in that house anymore. Is there room at the hotel next door?'

'No. They're fully booked with the people from the memorial.'

'Why don't you come and see if there's a room at the little hotel where we're staying?' Alex said. 'If not,

I'm sure you could bunk in with me. Harry can sleep on the floor of another room.' She looked at Harry, who nodded.

'I think it's a better idea than being in the house with Fenton and Zach,' he replied. 'Can you pack some things and come with us?'

'I can. I didn't bring a lot of stuff. We're only here for a few days, so I didn't bring a wardrobe with me. No need for an evening gown.'

'We can drive you anywhere you need to go,' Turnbull said. 'We have a spare car that can be used. The Wolf family always made sure we were wanting for nothing.'

'Good,' Dunbar said. 'Make the call and get the ball rolling, son.'

Turnbull nodded and walked back to the patrol car.

'That's not the same sergeant who was giving you lip earlier, surely?' Harry said as he looked at Turnbull's back.

'I had my DI, Tom Barclay, call him up and give him a roasting. Just making sure he didn't think I was some kind of pushover.'

'It did the trick,' Harry replied, then had a coughing fit.

TWENTY-ONE

'Can I get you a wee brandy?' Nancy Shaw said, coming into the bar. 'You both look like you're shaken up.'

'Thanks, that would be great, Mrs Shaw,' Dunbar said. 'I think we could all do with a wee drink. Stick it on the tab, will you?'

'Aye, of course.' She went behind the bar to pour the drinks. The bar was technically closed, with most of the other guests having departed, except for one old couple who were finishing up. Nancy brought some glasses out and poured the drinks, including one for herself.

'I think I'll be fine after a hot shower,' Harry said.

'Me too,' Missy said. She had a holdall at her feet, hurriedly packed when they had all gone back to the big house. Neither of the Wolf boys had been around and Thomas Deal had presumably gone to bed, probably long before sundown. There was no sign of Brian Gibbons.

They all took a drink. Harry felt the warmth of the liquid burning its way down and was grateful for it.

'You don't mind if Missy bunks in with Alex, do you?' Harry asked Nancy.

'No, of course not. You shouldn't be alone tonight.' She looked at Harry. 'Where are you going to sleep?'

Harry looked at Dunbar.

'Aw, look, neighbour,' Dunbar said, his head trying to come up with all sorts of reasons why Harry couldn't share his room, ranging from heavy snoring to having rickets.

'There is another wee room, next to Robbie's,' Nancy said. 'It's like a broom cupboard, but it's got a bed in it. You'd have to share a bathroom with some of the other guests.'

'That would be terrific, Nancy, thank you,' Dunbar said, grinning at Harry. 'Nothing personal, mucker.'

'Offence taken,' Harry replied.

'We'll be next to each other,' Evans said, as if this was a positive thing.

'Just do me a favour,' Dunbar said. 'Don't have a snoring competition.'

'I appreciate this, Mrs Shaw,' Missy said.

'No problem, love. I think this has put the wind up

everybody.' Nancy looked at her watch. 'I'm going to get the kettle on through the back for old Boxer. He likes a cup of tea before bed. Just give us a shout if you need anything.'

Nancy left the bar and they stood up, getting ready to go upstairs. The elderly couple walked by, and the old woman stopped and spoke to Harry.

'I couldn't help overhearing what you were talking about. The house going on fire on the north island. Nothing like this has happened on the island for a very long time.'

They all looked at her. 'What do you mean, "for a very long time"? It's happened before?' Harry said.

'Well, you know about Murdo Wolf. Went missing in his plane two days before Christmas, thirty-five years ago.'

They nodded their heads in unison, agreeing that they did indeed know what had happened, and his sudden reappearance was one of the reasons they were now sitting in a bar which would transform into a breakfast room later on.

'That's not the whole story. Two days before, a house belonging to the Wolf family burned to the ground.'

'Where was this?'

'You were in it tonight, love. It was the same house.'

TWENTY-TWO

'How do you feel this morning?' Alex said, coming into Harry's room.

'A bit stiff. But I've had a hot shower and feel much better. How about you? Miss me spooning with you?'

'Of course I did.'

'How did Missy sleep?'

'Well, we weren't spooning, if that's what you're insinuating.'

'I'm not. And don't play with Harry's head this early in the morning. Harry doesn't like it.'

'Tell Harry his wife doesn't like it when he talks like that. Alex thinks it's very irritating.'

'Okay. But how did Missy sleep?'

'Restless. She woke up a few times. Unlike us, the only dangerous thing she's done in her life is drink some milk that was a week past its sell-by date.'

'We could have both died in there last night. Whoever they are, they're not messing about.'

'Let's not try to stretch our brains too much. We damn well know who they are.' Her cheeks were starting to get a little bit red as anger touched them. 'Fenton fucking Wolf and his scabby brother, Zach. I am going to boot them in the bollocks when I see them. Try to kill my husband? Yeah, you have me to answer to now. Bastards.'

'It pleases me that you're so protective,' Harry said, 'but form a queue. I want them in the station today, answering some bloody questions.'

'It's the memorial today for Oliver Wolf.'

'Then they won't want to hang around. The quicker they answer, the quicker they can leave.'

'I suggested to Jimmy we go now.'

'Agreed. Has he had breakfast?'

'And spoken to his wife and dog. Robbie, I'm not too sure about.'

They left Harry's room and he knocked on Evans' door. No answer.

'He might be downstairs,' Alex suggested.

There was no sign of him, but Dunbar was sitting outside at a bench table with Missy. Then they saw Evans further along, on his phone.

'Morning, Harry. Alex. You had breakfast?'

'Just a quick coffee. I'm not that hungry. You?' Harry said.

'Same. I was up early. I got Missy here to do some checking on her iPad. After what that woman said last night about the house being burned down thirty-five years ago. Tell him what you found, Missy.'

Harry and Alex sat down at the table. The sun was out but was yet to make the island feel warm.

'I did some digging and public records show that the house didn't belong to Murdo Wolf. It belonged to Oliver.'

'Why is that strange?' Harry asked.

'All the other properties were owned by Murdo and only passed down to Oliver after Murdo was declared dead. That's not the strange thing, though; the twist is, Murdo burnt the house down.'

'Murdo?' Alex said.

'Yes. He was drunk and was just standing there watching the flames take hold of the property when the police and fire brigade arrived. He confessed, and was arrested, which meant they were just going through the motions. He was charged and released. An officer drove him home to sober up. The next morning, he had a lawyer. Nobody knows what the outcome would have been as he disappeared two days later.'

'People probably thought he had disappeared so he

wouldn't have to face up to his responsibilities,' Harry said.

Missy shrugged. 'Nobody knows why he did it, but there was plenty of speculation. They thought he was hurting for money and would claim the insurance money on it, but he got caught. However, from reading the police report, I don't think he wasn't trying to hide anything so I think there was something else entirely going on.'

'And now, almost thirty-five years later, somebody burns it down again,' Dunbar said. 'But this time, they were trying to elevate it to murder.'

'We're dealing with somebody more dangerous than anything else; somebody who doesn't care,' Alex said.

Harry shook his head. 'No. *Two* people who don't care. We're looking for a team.'

'Let's get along to the big house, neighbour. I want to be there when they reveal that the memorial is cancelled,' Dunbar said.

'The boys said it's going ahead,' Missy said.

'Surely to God they can't be serious?' Harry said to her.

'Let's go and talk to them,' Dunbar said.

TWENTY-THREE

'Fenton and Zachary?' Thomas Deal said, trying unsuccessfully to stifle a yawn. 'I haven't seen them yet, but you know young people; they like to lie about in bed all day.'

Harry turned to Alex and Evans. 'Could you both go and see if they're in their rooms? And Brian Gibbons.'

'Yes, sir,' Evans said, then he asked Deal which rooms to knock on.

They went upstairs and came back a few minutes later. 'Fenton and Zach aren't there. Brian said he'll get dressed and be down in a minute,' Alex said.

'Okay. Call Lillian Young and get her to liaise with the investigator to check out the burnt-out house as well.'

'I'm sure fire investigators will have that in hand.'

JOHN CARSON

'Wait, what?' Deal said. 'What burnt-out house?'

'The house that belonged to Clive. On the north side.'

'The log cabin?'

'Yes.'

'It's been burnt out?'

Harry nodded, watching the man's features. 'Somebody torched it last night. Missy and I were in it and we were attacked.'

The colour drained from Deal's face. 'Oh my God. Are you both okay?'

'We are, but it was a close thing. They were going to murder us and set the house on fire to cover their tracks, but we fought them off.'

'Them? There was more than one? Are you sure?'

'Of course I'm sure. I was there.' Harry's voice came out a bit harsher than he'd wanted it to, but somebody trying to kill him had that effect.

Deal sat down in a chair. 'Would you mind getting me a glass of water, dear?' he asked Missy, who left the living room and went through to the kitchen.

'Do you know why Murdo Wolf would burn the cabin down back in the day?' Dunbar asked.

Deal whipped his head round like he had been slapped. 'No! No, I wouldn't know why he did that. Murdo was under a lot of strain at the time. Oliver's wife was sick. She had been sick for a very long time and her long-term prognosis wasn't good. It was a very upsetting time for us. Plus his own wife had only been gone for a couple of years.'

'Yet he was still having the party?' Dunbar said.

'It had been arranged for a long time. Everybody loved coming to Murdo Wolf's parties, especially the Christmas party. No expense was spared. But that year it was going to be cancelled; Murdo insisted. Oliver was the one who wanted it to go ahead, not Murdo. He said it was what his wife would have wanted. It was the time of year that the staff got together too, and the Wolf family would show their appreciation. Murdo got upset, but Oliver had a meltdown and told the old man that the party was going ahead, with or without him.'

'And the party was the night Murdo disappeared,' Alex said. 'Or was murdered, I should say.'

'One of the parties, my dear,' Deal said, taking the glass of water from Missy after she appeared with it. 'There was a party almost every night.'

Harry was standing looking out of the window, trying to make sense of it all. Something had been niggling away at him, some little detail that kept appearing like a ghost through the mist, only to go away again before he could get a grip of it.

In the distance, a commuter plane was on its final approach to Laoch airport. He thought back to when he had been on the plane and wouldn't look down to the fairground.

Then it came to him. He turned back to the room.

'There's a plane coming in to land,' he said. 'Over there in the distance.'

'Yes,' Deal said.

'You told me that you knew Murdo was on the plane the night he took off because he got permission to take off.'

'Correct.'

'He would have had to have followed the corridor, or whatever it's called, the same flight path every other plane takes when it leaves here. On a different path the incoming planes take,' Harry said.

'Of course.'

Harry pinched the bridge of his nose for a moment. 'The planes don't fly too far out from the island, just in case of emergencies, so they can make it back to dry land. But enough distance separating each air corridor for obvious reasons. One flight path in, one out. Now, the air traffic controllers said the plane took the normal flight path, but then dropped off the radar. That's why they thought it went down into the sea and they could never find it, or Murdo.'

'Yes. But what's your point?' Deal said.

'It was something you said,' Harry continued. 'You

said you heard a plane coming over the house so low that you thought it was going to crash into it.'

Deal stared into space for a moment. 'Yes, I did.'

'Did anybody else hear it?'

Deal drank some more water. 'The drinks were flowing. If anybody else did, then they didn't say anything. It was mid-evening and people were already half-gassed.'

'What's your line of thinking here, Harry?' Dunbar said.

'If the plane flew out from the airstrip at the hotel next door, it would still have to fly onto the flight path. You saw it heading away from the hotel, didn't you?'

'Yes,' Deal said, 'I did. He was heading in the right direction.'

'Then how did he end up coming back over the hotel when he shouldn't have been anywhere near it?'

Deal didn't answer for a moment. 'I have no idea,' he said quietly.

'I'm assuming because he was so low, he would have been under the radar,' said Harry. 'Just like he was when he took off. But when he climbed, he was on the radar in the control tower. Then, when he dipped below it, he could have turned back and landed again. Just like he would have if he had picked up his friends from the mainland. Except he never got to the mainland. He turned around and flew straight back.'

'That doesn't make sense.'

'How long between him taking off and you hearing the plane come back over?' Dunbar asked.

Deal shrugged. 'Fifteen minutes maybe. I thought maybe he'd changed his mind, and was coming back because of the weather or something, but then he didn't appear so I thought it was maybe somebody else. Some other idiot flying a plane. Then I had a few drinks and didn't think about it again.'

'I don't think Murdo was flying the plane that night. Coming back, I mean. He might have taken off in it, but his killer was with him and his killer landed the plane,' Harry said.

'Why wouldn't he just have killed Murdo on the ground?' Deal asked.

'Despite the bad weather, there were a lot of people going about for the party. Somebody might have seen him. It was a lot easier for the killer to kill Murdo on the plane than on the ground.'

'So his killer took off with him, killed him in mid-air and brought him back?' Deal said.

'That's what I think. The question is, who killed him? And where could the plane have been hidden?'

TWENTY-FOUR

'What's all the commotion?' Brian Gibbons said as he walked into the living room.

'Where were you last night, Mr Gibbons?' Harry asked him.

'I had a few drinks here with Thomas, then I went to bed. Why?'

'Oh, nothing much. Just that somebody tried to kill me and Miss Galbraith.'

'What? Jesus Christ. I hope you don't think it was me?'

Harry looked at the man standing before him, dressed in sweatpants and a grubby tee shirt, and thought no, that wasn't the man who'd tried to attack him with a hammer. However, Brian had enough money to pay somebody to do it. What the motive would be, Harry didn't know yet.

'We'd like to talk to you in private,' Harry said. 'The kitchen should do.'

He and Dunbar followed the big man through.

'Jesus, this is getting worse,' Brian said, switching the kettle on. 'Shall I be Mother?'

'Sit down,' Dunbar said.

'I think better when I've sobered up. Let me tell you, that old boy can't half shift the drink. I thought I could put it away, but by God he has hollow legs.'

Dunbar got Harry to use the photo app on his phone to start recording. 'You didn't leave the house last evening?' Harry said as they sat down at the table across from Brian.

'No. Me and Tom sat and reminisced. Had a few whiskies. Then I had some beer. Actually, Tom was on the vodka. I don't know how he did it. I carry a few extra pounds and can absorb more, but by God he gave me a run for my money.'

'Neither of you left the house?'

Brian shook his head and gave a little laugh. 'Neither of us was in a fit state.'

'Missy said she didn't see anybody when she came in to get her things,' Harry said.

Brian shrugged. 'We were in the living room having a drink. Maybe that was after she came and went. How would I know? All I do know is that we were in here drinking.'

'How long were you married to Shona?' Dunbar asked.

Brian looked longingly at the kettle as it switched itself off. 'Just one cup. My head's buzzing and my throat feels like it's been slit.' He started to smile but then it fell off.

'Hurry up,' Dunbar said.

'You two want one?'

'No,' Harry said.

'I won't gob in it. It's only instant, but it's good stuff.'

'Just get on with it,' Dunbar said.

'Suit yourself.' Brian moved about the kitchen with finesse, like some overweight people move on the dance floor, but his particular partner was a carton of milk from the fridge.

'Right, there we are.' He sat down at the table and slurped some of the hot liquid. 'Oh, ya bastard. That's hot. Maybe I should put some more milk in.'

'Stay there,' Harry said. 'Now, again, how long were you married to Shona?'

Brian smiled. 'Too long.'

'What does that mean?' Harry said.

'I know it means you're looking at me through a different pair of eyes now, thinking that I was the one who ran into the car with that machine, but I wasn't. I don't know who it was, but I think they did me a favour.'

The detectives looked at each other before concentrating on Brian again.

'Oh, don't get me wrong, I was fond of Shona. Liked her a lot, actually. But as for love? Nah. I didn't love her one bit. And she didn't love me either.'

'How long were you married?' Dunbar said. 'If you can manage to give us a straight answer this time.'

'Less than a year. It was a marriage of pure convenience. We had an open marriage, you could say.'

'You're telling us a woman who wasn't even forty married an old geezer like you just for convenience?'

'That's it, my old son. Shona was only a few years off turning the big four-oh, and her daddy didn't want her to enter that stage of her life without a man on her arm. So that man was me. Bought and paid for.'

'Keep going,' Harry said as Brian blew on the surface of his coffee.

Brian took a sip and winced. 'Burnt my bloody lip there. For God's sake. I mean, how hot can coffee be?'

They waited for Brian to have another sip. 'I'm telling you this, never again. Especially with old Tommy boy there. He's a machine.' Another sip.

Harry was beginning to think Brian was stalling for time, but then the older man put the mug down and sat back in the chair.

'Now, you two fine gentlemen might think it's fun being married to a much younger woman. And it is. If it's the right woman. And Shona wasn't the right woman, not for me.'

'Why marry her then?'

'As I said, bought and paid for. It was Oliver's idea. Don't get me wrong, Shona and I got along just fine when we were in the company of her father, and we even had a few laughs when we were in the hotel bar, but that was it. I came here to talk business with Oliver, and he was giving it serious consideration. Hell, we even got as far as shaking on it one night. You know, a gentlemen's agreement?'

'But?' Dunbar said when Brian paused.

'But there was a caveat.' Brian picked up the mug and blew on the coffee again, then tentatively sipped the brew until he felt it was acceptable, if not quite chug-able.

'I knew the island well. My old man lived here when he was a lad, and I came here in my younger days. I saw the potential. All that land down by the shore. It would be tremendous to have nice houses there, with a private club and the marina near it. This is a terrific little place. The only fly in the ointment was Oliver Wolf. He owned the land. I wanted to build on it. But I didn't have the rights or the finances. Oliver did. So I suggested a partnership. My business finance was all tied up in other projects. Oliver had me over a barrel. Of course, he could have brought somebody else in, but not everybody would have been interested. And nobody would have been interested in marrying his daughter.'

'She was a widow,' Dunbar said. 'Why was he so interested in getting her married off again?'

'It was all about appearances with Oliver. His two oldest sons are divorced, but that was alright. It was almost like Fenton and Zach were in a macho club. Clive was fine too; the young man about town, sleeping with anything that had a pulse. But Shona was the little girl. Heading into old age on her own. It was like a slur on the family character for her not to have a husband.'

'No offence, but wasn't there anybody else Oliver could have got to marry his daughter?' Harry said.

'Cheeky sod. I might be some old, fat bastard, but I do very well for myself. Besides, as I said, Shona knew this was a sham marriage. She was used to being kept by Daddy. So he decided that if she didn't want to marry me, she would be cut loose and would have to make it on her own in the big, bad world. And he told me that if I didn't marry her, then there would be fuck all available to me regarding building on the island. And to be honest, I was in dire financial straits. Mortgaged up to the hilt. I'd had my car repossessed. My business was going down the toilet. So I agreed. Started going out with Shona.'

'It must have been hard for two people to go out just for convenience,' Dunbar said. 'I mean, I've heard of arranged marriages, but not in Scotland. By Scottish people, I mean.'

Brian drank more coffee. 'I was at a loose end anyway. And she was attractive enough, if you liked that sort of stuff. But there was never any physical contact, in the bedroom. In fact, we had separate bedrooms. It was a marriage on the outside, but we saw other people, just purely for physical needs.'

Harry was about to say something when Brian put up a hand to silence him. 'I know what you're thinking: who could possibly be interested in somebody like me? But trust me, not all women are as shallow as Shona Wolf was.'

'I was going to ask if her brothers knew about your marriage,' Harry said.

'Oh. Right. Well, not from me. I didn't think so, mind, but after the way Fenton mouthed off the other night, now I'm not so sure.'

'You know all of this could be looked on as a motive for murder,' Dunbar said.

Brian blew on the coffee again, not wanting to risk another burn to the lip. 'Why? I get nothing if she dies. That was a stipulation. Only things or money that we built up as a couple. Which we did, of course, but not much. I would keep the business interests that I started with Oliver, which wasn't a whole lot. I'll be lucky to come out of this with a pair of underpants to my name. Even the fucking car's wrecked. That was my car. The Range Rover we drove around in back home in Edinburgh was leased in the Wolf company name.'

'Who do you think would have it in for Clive and Shona?' Harry said.

Brian looked down into his coffee mug for a moment as if the answer were swirling about in the brown liquid. Then he looked first at Harry, then Dunbar. 'Look, I know this sounds bad, but me and Shona were arguing before she left to go back to the car.' He held up a hand even though nobody else was talking. 'Let me finish. She started accusing me of killing her brother. She said Clive had overheard somebody talking about where old Murdo was hidden. Clive was going off his nut, but he trusted Shona enough to tell her. They were twins after all. She started getting hysterical and paranoid. She turned around and headed back to the car.'

'Didn't you follow her?' Harry asked.

'Of course I did, but in case you haven't noticed, I'm not built like Eric Liddell. I tried to catch up, but by that time my knees were turning to jelly and what used to be a pair of lungs in my chest was two lumps of coal, well alight. So I thought, fuck it, and turned round and carried on back up the hill. At a more leisurely pace. I stopped at what would be known to a fat bastard like me as base camp, but what's more commonly known to other hikers as a picnic spot.'

'If I wasn't sitting here talking to you right now, I wouldn't believe it,' Dunbar said. 'But since we can see that you're not exactly on the Olympic cross-country team, I'm inclined to give you the benefit of the doubt.'

'Feel free to tell it like it is,' Brian replied.

'I will. That's what Police Scotland pay us for: to insult, cajole and otherwise mock anybody as we see fit, until we get a confession.'

Brian grinned and sat back, the mug and its contents now cool enough to cradle in one hand. He took a sip and looked at Dunbar. 'Sorry, but I'm going to have to disappoint you. I didn't kill Shona. But if it was true what Shona was saying, that Clive overheard people talking about Murdo's resting place inside that wall, maybe they knew he was going to look, so they killed him.'

'That's an avenue we're looking at,' Harry said.

'Did Shona say who it was that Clive overheard?' Dunbar asked.

Brian shook his head. 'No, but she was scared and paranoid. She thought I had something to do with it.'

'Did you believe her? About what Clive had said?'

'What reason would she have to lie? You didn't see her face when we were on the hill. It was like something had taken over her.'

'You didn't see anything suspicious when you parked the car?' Dunbar said.

'Nothing at all. Just an empty building site.'

Dunbar looked at Harry before looking back at Brian. 'That's enough for now, Mr Gibbons. But I am going to recommend to Thomas Deal that he cancels the memorial.'

'The boys won't be happy.'

'People have been murdered. There was an attempted murder. This party is one that the Wolf family are going to cancel.'

'Not my call. I couldn't care less. In fact, I'm going to pack, then I'm going home. While I still have one.'

'I can't let you do that,' Dunbar said.

'I don't want to turn my back on those two freaks. You ask me, the Wolf boys are the ones who killed their siblings. They're off their heads.'

Dunbar and Harry stood, and Brian followed suit.

'Thank you for your time, Mr Gibbons. Stick around,' Dunbar reiterated.

Back in the living room, Alex was talking with Thomas Deal. Robbie Evans came walking back in.

'Everything alright, son?' Dunbar said, taking him aside.

'I got a text, telling me it was urgent. From Bernadette. I couldn't get hold of her this morning. I didn't think she had left to go on holiday yet. I normally don't answer texts when I'm at work, but I thought –'

'That's fine, Robbie. Tell me what's going on.'

Evans looked uncertain for a moment. 'Her husband sent me a text, telling me to stay away from his wife.'

'Ah, shite. Sorry, son.'

Evans looked grim. 'You were right, though. I almost made a right arse of myself.'

'A right arse cheek, if I remember correctly.'

Evans gave a grim smile.

'It happens to the best of us,' Dunbar said.

'But it happened to me. Bloody hell. Maybe I should just become a monk.'

'Not today, though. We have some bastards we want to talk to. Including those Wolf muppets.'

'Aye. Tomorrow then.'

TWENTY-FIVE

Thomas Deal was sitting reading a newspaper in the living room, certainly not in the same state as Brian Gibbons.

'We have a lot on today,' he said, folding the newspaper and standing up. 'Oliver's friends will be champing at the bit to say their goodbyes.'

'There's not going to be a memorial,' Dunbar said. 'It's too dangerous. We can't guarantee everybody's safety.'

'This is preposterous. I won't hear of it.'

'You have no choice, Mr Deal,' said Harry. 'People tried to kill us last night, and they're still out there. Those two men are very dangerous.'

'Two men?' Deal said.

'Yes,' Harry said. 'Now, can you tell us where Fenton and Zachary might be?'

'They don't check in with me, but they might be at Fenton's house, the one his father left him.'

'Which is where?'

'It's on the other side of the loch from the house Clive was left. The road that forks to the right and goes to Clive's house? Go past that. There's a road on the left off the main road. It goes up into the hills and has a view of the loch from the other side. It's a beautiful property. You can't miss it. It's called Hillside.'

Just then, Crail Shaw walked in. 'Some of the guests are in the dining room at the hotel, talking about the memorial. Some of them have expressed an interest in leaving soon. What do you want me to tell them?'

Deal looked at Dunbar before answering. 'Tell them there's not going to be a memorial. Due to Clive's and Shona's deaths. It wouldn't be appropriate. Something like that. Tell them we'll hold a memorial in Edinburgh sometime in the near future.'

'Very good, sir.' Crail looked at the detectives before leaving again.

'I didn't know Crail still worked for the Wolf family,' Harry said.

'Boxer? He's worked for the family for a very long time. Ever since I met Oliver he's been a part of the fixtures. He does maintenance for the hotel.'

'Have you ever gone boxing with him down at the carnival?' Dunbar asked.

'Do I look like the sort of man who goes fighting, Chief Inspector?'

'He must keep himself fit.'

'I think he does. But he has his wife to look after their own hotel.'

'Oh, yes. He was left that hotel after Murdo was declared dead, wasn't he?'

'He was. A token of Murdo's appreciation. And Oliver's too.'

Outside, Harry drew in a deep breath of air. 'Maybe we should take back-up?'

'There're two schools of thought on that one. First, there might be nothing there. Second, we have Robbie the Rottweiler with us.' Dunbar looked at Evans. 'Don't look so glum. You'll find somebody else.'

'You been dumped already?' Harry asked.

'Och. Why don't you just announce it over the airwaves?'

Dunbar grinned. 'Looking for this Wolf pair will surely cheer you up. You never know, you might get to skelp one of them.'

'Maybe we should take Muckle with us?' Alex said.

'He's technically a civilian,' said Dunbar, 'so we can't put him at risk. As much as I'd like him to tag along.'

They got in the replacement car and drove out

along the coast road. Alex hung a left when they came to a sign for a place called *Teach sa Speir*.

'It's Gaelic for *House in the sky*,' Evans said.

'I'm impressed you knew that,' Dunbar said.

'According to Google.' Evans held his phone up.

'Just when I think you're halfway intelligent, you go and spoil the illusion.'

The road was narrow and windy until it came into a clearing. The house faced west, with the back facing east, and the loch below.

'The Wolf family certainly knew how to look after themselves,' Evans said.

'Wouldn't you? If you had their kind of money?' Dunbar said. 'I would. Nice big garden for Scooby to run about in, a nice motor that wouldn't get us stuck when it snowed.'

'Must be nice.'

'There are no cars here, that I can see,' Alex said, coming to a halt in front of the house.

'Just be on your guard,' Harry said. 'If these are the pair who attacked me and Missy last night, then they're not playing about.'

'We'll watch ourselves, neighbour,' Dunbar said.

They got out of the car and could see the dark clouds in the distance, rolling towards them. 'I don't think we should linger,' Dunbar said. 'Robbie, go round the back of the house, son. Give us a shout if either of those reprobates makes a run for it.'

Evans left them and walked round the back of the big house. It was made of dark-grey stone and blended in with the hillside.

The door was ajar and Harry nudged it wide open. It felt like walking into the lion's den. They heard a noise from the back, but it was only Evans.

They searched together in case they were attacked, but after a few minutes it was clear that the house was empty.

'No sign that they've even been here,' Harry said as they went back outside.

He looked over to the ocean in the distance. This house had a view of the loch at its back and the ocean at its front. Whoever had built the house had known what they were doing.

He watched as another plane flew in from the coast, heading towards the airport. He imagined Murdo Wolf taking off with his killer, then dying on the plane, and the killer swinging the small aircraft round and heading back inland, flying right across the hotel.

He could see the carnival and fairground in the distance, and the big house further along. The hotel was down a bit from it. As his eyes followed the path that the plane would have taken, he wondered where it had gone after that. Obviously, it had landed somewhere. But where? It was hard to tell from this place. He couldn't make out any long, flat piece of land. He looked further along, seeing nothing until...he saw something.

'What's that?' he said, pointing.

'A big, dirty cloud, mucker,' Dunbar said, coming to stand beside him.

'There, through those trees in the distance.'

Dunbar squinted. 'I can't see anything but trees. My eyes aren't what they used to be.'

'It looks like a building. I can see a bit of a turret or something. Poking up above the trees. See it?'

'I can barely see the rollercoaster down at the fairground and that goes up into the air.' Dunbar turned towards Evans. 'Robbie! Get your eyes over here.'

'My eyes?'

'Aye. Look over in that direction. What do you see?'

Evans looked. 'The sea?'

'I'll chuck you in the fucking sea in a minute. Over there. To the right. Where the trees are on that hill.'

'Oh, right. That turret thing. I see it now.'

Dunbar looked at him. 'Do you really, or are you taking the piss?'

'No, I see it. In amongst those trees.'

Dunbar gave him a look that suggested a bollockkicking might be in order should the younger sergeant be winding him up.

'Why don't you call Muckle and see if he knows what it is?' Alex suggested.

'Good idea.' Dunbar took his phone out. But there were no bars on it. 'Shite. No service up here.'

'I'm sure there has to be a road leading to it. We know what direction it's in, so we could try to find the road leading to it and check it out.'

Dunbar nodded. 'Good idea. Why didn't you think of that?' he said to Evans. 'Get yer heid out of your arse.'

They got back in the car and drove down to the main road and turned right, heading in what they thought was the direction of the house.

The bars came back on the phone. 'Bloody phones,' Dunbar said, dialling Muckle's number.

'Listen, mate, we saw a house in the trees in the middle of nowhere. Near the house that Fenton Wolf was left by his old man. Any idea what it is?'

'I've not got a clue. Hold on, I'm at the hotel. Missy Galbraith asked me to come along, in case there was any trouble.'

'I thought you didn't work for the Wolf family anymore?'

'I heard what happened last night. This is just a favour for her. Hold on, I'll see if she knows.'

Dunbar could hear muffled talking and then Muckle came back on the line. *'She says she's never been to it, and it isn't part of the will or anything, but it's an old house belonging to the Wolf family, right enough. It's called Hillside. But get this: it was an asylum.'*

'An asylum?' Dunbar looked at Harry and made a face.

He could hear Muckle being spoken to again. Then the man came back on the line.

'Aye. It wasn't just an asylum. It was a proper wee hospital, but it had a small psychiatric wing. The new hospital opened, and services transferred there, but Murdo Wolf kept his wife locked up. She'd had a breakdown and he kept her there, with staff looking after her. It was closed after his wife died. It's been closed up for years now and never reopened. Not since Murdo died.'

'Thanks, pal.' Dunbar cut the call and told the others what Muckle had just told him. 'Seems old Missus Wolf was the sole psychiatric patient in that big hoose. It was a hospital.'

'There has to be a road somewhere nearby,' Harry said.

'Up there, on the right,' Evans said, looking back down at his phone.

'Your eyes *are* sharp,' Dunbar said from the back

seat. 'Despite your mother telling you you'll go blind one day.'

'I have Google Maps up on my phone.' Evans added something under his breath.

'What was that?'

'Blind and deaf,' Evans said to Alex as she turned the car onto the narrow road.

'I bloody well heard that, though.' Dunbar resisted the urge to smack Evans on the back of the head. 'This better be right. Bloody Maps. Give me a good old road map any day. What do you say, Harry?'

'I don't know, Jimmy, these things are kind of handy on your phone.'

'Until you can't get any bars or your phone dies. Aye, exactly. I don't hear a peep out of any of you.'

The gates were across the road and nature had started to take the hillside back. Trees and bushes lined the path, and the tarmac had long since given up trying to keep itself together. Big cracks allowed weeds to creep through.

Alex stopped and they sat looking at the gates.

'They're not going to bloody open themselves,' Dunbar said.

Alex and Evans got out and walked up to the wrought-iron gates. Evans lifted the iron peg that was keeping one of the gates closed, and it slid up easily.

He moved the gate in and it offered no resistance. Alex moved the other one.

'No, no, that's alright, we got it,' Evans said, getting back in the car.

'Good, because I had no intention of lifting my arse off this seat,' said Dunbar.

Alex grinned as she got back behind the wheel. The tyres crunched over broken tarmac and what looked like either small bushes or huge weeds.

'Seriously, though, boss, that gate moved like it was opened every day. I was expecting to have to shove it hard, but it almost glided.'

The road went through a canopy of trees for almost a quarter of a mile before breaking out into a wide driveway. There was an old car park over on the right, empty now except for more weeds. It had been mostly gravel at one time before the greenery got hold of it.

The house was on three levels with a tower on the left-hand side, poking through the trees. More modern wings had been tacked on to the side, extending it.

Dunbar took his phone out, but once again the bars had disappeared. 'Christ, why are we paying so much every month for service that's little better than two cans and a piece of string?' he said.

Alex stopped the car in front of the main doors, and they got out. Miraculously, none of the windows were broken, except one, where a branch had been blown through it. Apparently, Laoch didn't have an abundance of vandals. Or maybe they just didn't want to come up to the old asylum.

There were old lampposts, but Harry doubted they were working. Why would they waste electricity lighting up an old building that had been abandoned for years?

'I wonder why this place wasn't mentioned by any of the Wolf brats?' Harry said as Alex and Evans wandered off to one side.

'Who knows?' Dunbar said. 'Maybe they're just embarrassed by this place. But it will get sold anyway. If anybody wants to buy an old asylum.'

'If this was Edinburgh, it would have been torn down by now and flats built on it.'

'Look over here,' Harry said. He walked over to an iron gate set into a stone wall. It opened easily. He and Dunbar walked through into a small cemetery. There were only a few headstones in the small area. Harry stopped in front of a small row.

'Oliver Wolf and his wife,' Dunbar said.

'And Murdo Wolf. They must have put the stone up while he was still alive. There's no death date. And his wife next to him.'

'They'll be able to add the death date now, Harry.'

Harry nudged Dunbar. 'Look at the names. Murdo and Oliver.'

Dunbar looked at what Harry was pointing to and then he understood. They walked back out.

'See this!' Alex said, waving them over.

Harry and Dunbar walked over to where the new addition was attached to the old house. Alex pointed to an old sign that was sitting on the ground outside a set of double doors. Harry read it out loud.

'Accident and Emergency.' He looked at the others. 'This was the original Laoch hospital right enough.'

'Until they built the new one down on the south island,' Alex said.

'Which must have been before Murdo's wife died. She was the only one in here at the time.'

'I wonder how true that is,' Dunbar said. 'You know how rumours spread.' Again he gave Evans a look, and the younger detective just shook his head and looked away.

'I wonder why he didn't just move his wife down there?' Harry said.

'Maybe it was embarrassing for Murdo to admit his wife had mental health problems,' Dunbar said. 'It was all about appearances with the Wolf family. Like Oliver wanting his daughter to be married, even if it was to the Hunchback of Notre Dame.'

'It would make sense for him not to do anything with this place if he was grieving,' Alex said.

'I wonder how long she'd been dead before he died?' Evans said.

'Didn't old Deal say the wife died a few months before Murdo?' Dunbar said.

'I think so,' Harry replied.

The windows were filthy and it was clear nobody had been here in a long time. They walked down the side of the hospital until they were at the back.

'I think we should get back down, neighbour,' Dunbar said.

'Hold on a minute, Jimmy,' Harry said.

'What are you thinking, Harry?'

'It was when we were up at the other house. I saw a plane coming in to land again. I followed the line of sight from the airport, then the line that Murdo, or his killer, might have taken. Being a small aircraft, it could have landed almost anywhere, if he could find a piece of flat land.'

'That's true, but we might never know where he landed.'

Harry turned to look at Dunbar. 'Let's think about what we know about that night. It was snowing like it was the Arctic, according to Thomas Deal. Yet Murdo took off in it. Because the airstrip had been cleared.'

'Okay.'

'It was bucketing down with snow and visibility

was bad. The killer wouldn't risk flying around trying to find somewhere to land in the heavy snow.'

'Agreed.'

'He had to know where to land in advance. It was somebody who knew this island like the back of his hand. Somebody who knew where a makeshift airstrip was.'

Harry swept one arm open and they all turned to look at the back lawn of the hospital. A long, flat area of grass.

'Now it's overgrown, but thirty-five years ago it would have been a well-kept lawn.'

Dunbar looked at Evans. 'Go with Alex and get Muckle. And his big fuckin' dug. Get him to come up here and bring some uniforms. I want this place searched.'

'Got it, boss.'

The two sergeants ran back to the car and jumped in, then threw gravel as they sped away.

Harry watched the car until it disappeared. Then he looked at the road.

'There's something bothering me,' he said, walking right round the back of the building.

'What's that, neighbour?'

'That road we came up. The gates make the entrance narrow.'

'They do.'

'So where did the delivery trucks come in? And was that the ambulance entrance? I mean, this place wasn't like Edinburgh on a Friday night, I'm sure, but remember the fairground was here and our landlady at the hotel, Nancy, told us that this island is jumping with tourists.' Harry looked around. 'This hospital needed to have the Accident and Emergency because of the sheer number of visitors. I'm sure it was pretty busy, just like I'm sure the new one is busy, especially in the summer.'

'I'm following you,' Dunbar said. 'There has to be a service road. Big enough to take delivery trucks.'

'Correct.'

They reached the back of the big house, where a large extension had been added. Although the road was overgrown, it could still be made out.

'There it is.'

'Which means they could bring big vehicles in here. Including a snow plough. The hospital was already closed on the day that Murdo was murdered, so maybe the killer came up here and ploughed it in preparation.'

Dunbar nodded. 'Where would he have put the plane? I mean, he could have left it out in the open, but this killer is a planner. I don't think he would have risked just leaving the plane in view. He would have hidden it.'

'That's what I would have done. Then he could have come back and flown it out.'

'That would have been risky, neighbour. Even if he waited until spring, there was a chance of him being spotted. Not to mention popping up on radar. I know he flew in here under the radar, but that's not to say he wouldn't have been spotted by another plane. If I was him, I would have hidden it.'

'Me too. Then I would have dismantled it, bit by bit.'

They looked around and started walking away from the hospital, further along what they now thought of as the airstrip. There was a small copse of trees at the end. The grass was overgrown around it, but the service road followed the edge of the airstrip and bent round the edge of the copse.

Then they saw them. The outlying buildings. Sheds. And a garage with a double door. It was old, made of wood, but it was in decent enough condition. The glass panels had been covered with wood from the inside. Hidden from view by the trees and vegetation; more aesthetic for the patients.

'It's locked,' Harry said, trying the handle that would have opened one of the doors outwards. Dunbar looked round the side.

'There's a solid door there, but it's locked tight.'

The building was large and looked like it could

have stored a few double-decker buses, never mind gardening equipment and a snow plough.

'There has to be a way in,' Harry said.

'Let me look round the other side.' Dunbar walked away and disappeared from view, and just for a moment, Harry had an uneasy feeling. He followed in Dunbar's footsteps and turned the corner.

Dunbar wasn't there.

'Jimmy?'

Then Dunbar poked his head out from a doorway. 'Apparently, this door swings open and some bastard kicked it in.' He rubbed his knee and made a face. 'Where's young Robbie when you need him?'

Harry walked up and couldn't see much in the gloom. He took his phone out, but the little flashlight didn't illuminate much inside beyond the shaft of light pouring in from the doorway.

They stepped further in and their eyes adjusted more to the darkness.

Old machinery was piled everywhere. An old truck with a Leyland badge on the front sat facing the double doors. It had once been red, but it looked old and rusty now, like it had bled out and died a long time ago. It had a flat bed and old machinery was piled on it. A snow plough was over to one side and they could see the attachment on the front of the truck where the plough would have been put on in the winter.

'Bingo,' Dunbar said.

'This looks like it. Maybe the Wolf family bought it from the local council to keep their airstrip clear in the winter. Who knows?'

They walked round the side of the truck, where there was more scrap metal. It was like a scavenger's dream come true. There was a pathway between the junk and they walked back into the darkness, which wasn't totally pitch black. They could see a tarpaulin stretched over the top of something.

Harry looked down and saw the front wheel sticking out, its tyre flat. He nudged Dunbar.

'I think we just found Murdo Wolf's plane.'

They walked tentatively past the metal junk, careful not to tear their clothes or their skin. The whole place smelled musty and oily.

Junk had been placed on the wings, maybe in a clumsy attempt to disguise its shape should anybody ever have a quick peek in here, but it was obvious what it was up close.

Another tarpaulin covered the cab. Harry squeezed by some old machines and reached out to grab hold of the plastic sheet and he pulled.

Two faces stared back at them.

TWENTY-SIX

Zachary and Fenton Wolf looked back at them with dead eyes. Both of them had had their heads split open with what Harry could only imagine was a hammer.

'Jesus Christ, all the Wolf kids are dead,' Dunbar said, looking back at the plane.

'Not quite,' said a figure from the shadows.

'What the hell are you doing here?' Harry said to Crail Shaw.

'What do you think, Harry?' Dunbar said. 'The bastard's come to finish off the job.'

Boxer smiled in the darkness. Harry took a step towards him, the flashlight from his phone still glinting off some of the metal that wasn't rusty.

'You killed Murdo all those years ago,' Harry said matter-of-factly.

'I did. He was an old bastard. I worked for him, worked so damn hard, going the extra mile, but he treated me like shit.'

'That was no reason to kill him,' Dunbar said.

Boxer laughed loudly. 'You dumb fuck. That wasn't the reason I killed him. But the why doesn't concern you.'

'You were a pilot, obviously,' Harry said.

'Ironically, it was Murdo who taught me to fly. I never did get my pilot's licence, which helped because when they did a search back in the day, wondering if it really was Murdo in the plane, nobody else had a pilot's licence. But yes, I used to fly the plane with Murdo all the time. Oliver didn't, because he was shit-scared of the small planes, but I loved it. It's easy when you know how.'

'You took him up in the plane and killed him, then flew it back here,' Harry said.

'Correct. I had planned it well, making sure the snow was cleared off the airstrip, or the back lawn as the hospital called it. It was perfect for landing the small plane.'

'The *why* is irrelevant now anyway,' Dunbar said as they walked into the clear space in front of the truck. 'You're under arrest.'

He stepped forward, taking his handcuffs out of a

pocket, and was about to slap a cuff on one of Boxer's wrists when the older man hit him with a left hook. Dunbar went down hard, hitting the hard-packed floor.

'Jimmy!' Harry said, rushing forward to check on his friend, keeping an eye on Boxer at the same time.

Boxer stepped forward and tried to punch Harry, but Harry knew it was coming and ducked, jabbing Boxer in the face with a right fist. It was enough to knock the man back, and suddenly all the frustrations Harry had felt over the months rushed out. His ex-wife trying to keep his son from him; his mother's murder; people trying to kill him.

Boxer grinned and moved in with a classic boxer's stance and tried jabbing at Harry, but Harry was having none of it. He sidestepped and punched Boxer hard in the face. The older man was stunned, and Harry moved in, pummelling him with his fists, until the man fell back onto the floor.

'Enough! I've had enough, please.' Boxer lay still, his breath coming fast now, blood pouring from his mouth and nose. 'You win.'

Harry turned away and bent down to see that Jimmy was doing okay and still breathing.

'Fucking drop it!' a voice suddenly shouted.

Harry looked up and saw Muckle McInsh standing just inside the doorway. He also saw Boxer had silently got back up on his feet and was standing with a hammer in his hand, holding it up like he was going to strike with it.

'You big piece of shit,' Boxer said. 'I'll kill you after I've killed this pair.'

'I said fucking drop the hammer.'

Boxer smiled through the blood pouring out of his mouth. 'Who's going to fucking make me? You?'

'No. Jesus will. Fuckwit.'

Boxer saw the distance between himself and Muckle and knew he wouldn't be able to rush the man, so he turned his attention to Harry and Dunbar instead.

'Harry, down!' Muckle said, and as he brought his arm round, Harry didn't think twice about throwing himself down on top of Dunbar.

The shot rang out in the darkness and the buckshot caught Boxer in the chest before he could bring down the hammer. He flew backwards and landed on his back, the life ebbing out of him.

Muckle ran over, not turning his back on Boxer, and took the hammer from him.

Dunbar groaned. 'Look at you. You've not even taken me for a meal and a drink yet.'

'Aye, you fucking wish,' Harry said, getting to his feet. 'Get your fucking self up.'

He looked at Muckle. 'Good shot, pal.'

'I'll have some explaining to do, but at least I have a licence for it.'

'Where's your boy?' Dunbar said, getting up and rubbing his jaw.

'I wasn't going to bring him in here, not while I've got Jesus. I was already on my way here when Alex called.'

'Good call.'

'But he'll have ripped the seat of my car all to fuck and the wife will go nuts, so I'd better go see him.'

'That bastard,' Dunbar said, nodding to Boxer. 'He killed those Wolf boys and shoved them in the plane. Chances are, they might not have been found for a very long time.'

'One thing's puzzling me,' Harry said.

'What's that?'

'When I said, that's all the Wolf kids dead, he said, *not quite*. What did he mean by that?'

'No idea, neighbour. We still don't know why he killed Murdo.'

'I think I might know who does. Somebody we're already familiar with.'

'Brian Gibbons?'

Just then the cavalry arrived, a little too late, but there nonetheless. Evans came in with Alex and some uniforms were getting the double doors open, flooding the place with light.

'Don't get too comfortable. We have to go and speak to somebody,' Harry said, nodding to the corpse of Crail Shaw. 'This isn't over.'

TWENTY-SEVEN

Brian Gibbons was sitting having a drink in the living room. The only difference was, he was better dressed this time.

'What's going on?' he said. 'Everybody's going crazy. First the guests are not happy that the memorial's been cancelled, and now there're rumours you've caught my wife's killer.'

'There's more to it, Mr Gibbons,' Harry said.

'What's that supposed to mean? You don't think I killed her, do you? I mean, if you do, then you're barking up the wrong tree.'

'I did have my suspicions. However...where's Thomas Deal?'

'He was here a minute ago. His feathers have really been ruffled. He's strutting about like his head is going to fall off.'

'Where were you when you asked Missy about the old hospital?' Harry asked Muckle.

'In here.'

Harry nodded, and they heard raised voices outside the living room, then Thomas Deal walked in with Missy.

'Oh. You're here,' Deal said.

'Yes, we are,' Harry said.

'You got those painkillers?' Dunbar asked, and Alex pulled a pack from her pocket and popped two for Dunbar.

'I'll need a glass of water to wash those down with,' he said.

'I'll get one from the kitchen,' she said.

'No need.' He walked over to the drinks cabinet, picked up the bottle of vodka, poured a healthy measure into a glass and washed the two tablets down.

'Is that wise? Drinking on duty, sir?' Alex said.

Dunbar smiled as everybody in the room watched him. 'Don't worry, it's only water. Even though there's a vodka label on the bottle, it's only tap water.'

'I don't understand,' Brian Gibbons said.

Thomas Deal was about to leave the room, but Muckle McInsh blocked the doorway with Sparky, who was about ready to have lunch.

'You were drinking with Mr Deal last night, Mr Gibbons, but Deal was only drinking water. He pretended to be drunk so you could alibi him. He was helping Crail Shaw kill Fenton and Zachary.'

'Now, look...' Deal said. 'This is nonsense. He saw me drinking.'

'I was drinking whisky,' said Brian. 'I knew I was drunk. You looked like you were drunk.'

'That's surprising,' Harry said. 'Since you told us, Deal, that you didn't drink.'

Deal looked at them, then rushed at Muckle, but Sparky turned on the old man in a second. Deal stopped and threw himself against the wall.

'Get that dog away from me!' he shouted.

'He's just protecting me, fucking doughnut.'

'Don't talk to me like that.'

'Shut up and sit down,' Dunbar said.

The old solicitor did as he was told, not taking his eyes off the snarling dog.

'Now, Boxer said something to me before he died,' Harry said. 'I saw the two Wolf sons dead in that plane we found. But when I made a comment about all the Wolf kids being dead, he said, *not quite*. What did he mean by that?'

'I have no idea.' Deal sat back in the couch and folded his arms. 'I want a solicitor.'

'You're not under arrest. Yet. But let me tell you what I think, and feel free to jump in anytime to correct me if I'm wrong. I think there are still Wolf offspring out there.'

'How can that be?' Brian said, interrupting. 'Clive, Shona, and now, you said, Fenton and Zach. Oliver didn't have any more kids.'

Harry smiled and looked at Deal. 'That's not quite true, is it, Thomas?'

'I'm saying nothing. You'll never prove anything.'

'That's true.' Harry turned to face the small audience, and even Sparky was listening to him now. 'However, I don't think either you or Crail Shaw killed the Wolf kids. I think somebody else did. You see, you have to ask yourself, who benefits? Normally, if a parent dies, the child benefits. But not the Wolf kids. And I say kids, even though they're adults. They're Oliver Wolf's kids. Wait a minute, if they're all dead, then who benefits? The community? Maybe. If they're all out of the way, then there has to be somebody who would gain from it. That's you, Thomas. You're the one who will benefit.'

'You're talking nonsense.'

'Really? Let's ask Missy then, shall we?' He turned to Missy. 'Who benefits if the Wolf kids are dead?'

She nodded to Deal. 'He does.'

Harry turned back to him. 'You do. And Missy knew that. But what if she was out of the way? She couldn't tell anybody then, could she? That's why you tried to kill her last night. I don't think they expected me, but you sent them to kill her. Did you tell Fenton and Zach that if they killed her, they could split the extra money?'

A brief smile played over Deal's face before he looked at Harry. 'No, that was all their idea.'

'But you have to admit that with them out of the way you get everything. I mean, you helped Oliver draft his will, didn't you?'

'I did, but it was all above board.'

'I'm sure it was, because he didn't think the chances of you surviving his kids was remotely possible. And you thought that too, so you concocted the idea to have them all killed.'

'I'm saying nothing more.'

The room fell silent. Sparky lay down on his side, obviously bored with the proceedings, but ever attentive.

'We had the pathologist look at Fenton and Zach,' said Harry. 'They were dead before we were attacked in that house last night. It wasn't them who attacked us.'

'Then I don't know who did. I want to go and have a lie-down.'

'You do that, Mr Deal, but remember this: you'll be having a permanent lie-down soon.'

'Are you threatening me?'

Harry smiled. 'Oh no, I'm warning you. They're ruthless. They've killed without blinking an eye because they had their eye on the prize: the Wolf fortune. What do you think they'll do when they find out you conned them out of that fortune? That they killed for nothing? That they killed the people who were standing in *your* way? You think they'll just walk away?'

Dunbar walked over to Deal. 'We can't prove anything, but this is what we're thinking. Murdo somehow found out that he had another grandchild. Or grandchildren. He was going to tell Oliver he knew. He had to be stopped. You had Crail Shaw kill him and hide his body. But it was a two-man effort to put him in the wall in the new extension that was being built, so *you* helped him. It wasn't any of the kids, as they were too young. No, it took two adults to do that.'

'You're making up stories,' Deal snarled at him.

'Who did Clive Wolf overhear arguing before he died? You and Boxer? Was it Boxer you sent after him? I think Clive was smashing the wall and Boxer came in and killed him. But then you somehow got distracted and couldn't get Clive or Murdo out of there, and Muckle then found them.'

'How are we doing?' Harry said. 'Did you kill Murdo back then? Did Boxer? Was that what Clive overheard you arguing about?'

'Clutching at straws is what they call it,' Deal said, relaxing again.

'You think because we can't prove any of this that it will go away, but let me tell you something: the killers aren't going away. I think when they find out about you diddling them, they're going to come after you. They've nothing to lose now. They've already killed four people. What's another old man who might only have a few years left anyway? You think you'll live long enough to spend your money?'

'Oh, I think I'll take my chances.' Deal chuckled. 'You want me to give you names, is that it? Well, sorry to disappoint you.'

'That's fine. We'll leave you alone now.' Harry turned to Dunbar. 'Alex and I are going to the fairground. I think I'll have a wee chat with Jack Shaw. He's going to be upset that Boxer won't be around to challenge the public. He's a real showman is Jack. I'll break the news to him that his dad is dead, and if he asks me about things, I'll have to tell him he's getting nothing. But I can't prove anything, so I can't arrest him. He'll be free to go about the island as he pleases.'

'You do that, Harry,' Dunbar said. 'Meantime, I'll see if young Brendan will open the bar for me. I'll be needing a stiff drink after what I've been through. I'm sure Brendan's a good listener. And he'll be more than happy to listen to what I have to say.'

They'd started to leave the room when Deal sighed. 'Okay. You win.' He looked at both men. 'You bastards knew, didn't you?'

'Suspected. When I looked at the wills of Oliver and Murdo, I saw their middle names were Brendan and Jack. Just like Oliver's illegitimate sons. Am I right?'

Deal nodded. 'Murdo was going to announce it at the Christmas party. He was pissed off at Oliver, and he'd kept it from his late wife, but it was eating him alive. He wanted the world to know he had two more grandsons. Boxer – Crail – was furious. His wife was pregnant when he met her, but he decided to stand by her. He would bring them up as his own. Nancy told him she didn't know who the father was. Or he was dead, something like that. You've met Nancy; she's a nice woman. She adored the boys and she loved Boxer. Now Murdo was going to throw a spanner in the works. The boys were only a couple of months old at the time.'

'You knew Boxer killed Murdo?' Dunbar said.

'No. I suspected. He was the last one with Murdo. And I knew that Murdo had shown Boxer how to fly the plane. Boxer was a natural. I thought he had killed the old man, but I didn't know for sure. Until I confronted him years later. I told him that his boys deserved to get some of the Wolf money. He told me that Oliver had told him that all four of his kids would be taken care of. Bragging about it. But there was no mention of Boxer's sons. I told Boxer that Oliver was the father of his sons but still they were getting nothing. I confirmed this when Oliver died. I think Crail killed him. He was arguing with Oliver the night he died. Two days before Christmas, just like Murdo. I think Crail was thinking back to when he killed Murdo and he had it out with Oliver. But Oliver had a weak heart. He died of a heart attack, brought on by the stress of the fighting, I presume.'

'Then you, in effect, got the boys to kill the other kids for you so you would get everything,' Harry said. 'You decided to con them.'

'Pretty much. When I saw I was getting nothing either. I'd worked hard for the Wolf family over the years and was like a brother to Oliver. I was the one who got him out of all his little scrapes.'

'And now it's all for nothing. Let's go and get the Crail twins. And Alex? Arrest him before we go.'

TWENTY-EIGHT

The plan was to approach Jack Shaw without much fanfare, but have back-up just in case. Harry didn't want to flood the fairground with police. That would just alert the killer.

The idea was to converge on the boxing booth from both sides. There was already a crowd of people making the best of the good weather. The sun was out overhead, the wind was light and there was a definite feel-good mood amongst the crowds as early evening approached.

It was hard to believe that they were there to arrest a serial killer.

Jack Shaw was standing around, looking at his watch, when Harry approached. The young man was dressed in his showman's garb and had an annoyed look on his face.

'He's not coming,' Harry said. Alex sidled up on his other side.

Jack looked at Harry. 'Who are you?'

'I think you know full well who I am. We met last night. Was it you who had the hammer?'

Jack made a face and took his phone out, about to walk away.

'I already told you your dad isn't coming. He's dead.'

This got Jack's attention and he turned to look at Harry. 'What are you talking about?'

'We know all about the fact he killed Murdo Wolf all those years ago. And how Thomas Deal got you to kill for him. Did you know Deal was the beneficiary? He made sure that was the case if all the Wolf children were dead. He got you and your brother to kill them, thinking you were going to get the inheritance. You were getting nothing.'

'You're a fucking liar!' Jack said, instead of denying everything.

'Jack Shaw, I'm arresting you for the murder –' Harry started to say, but Jack dropped his phone and took up a boxer's stance.

'I don't think so.'

He was about to take a swing at Harry, but Harry had had enough. He stepped in close and head-butted

Jack on the bridge of the nose. Then Alex and Evans were all over Jack as he fell to the ground.

The crowds were starting to gather, thinking this was part of the show. Harry watched as Alex handcuffed Jack and they dragged him to his feet.

'Read him his rights, Sergeant,' Harry said to her.

Jack Shaw went quietly.

TWENTY-NINE

Nancy Shaw was in the dining room, setting up for dinner, when Dunbar and Evans walked in. Harry had gone to the station with Alex to book Jack Shaw in. This time, uniforms were waiting outside the small hotel.

'Hello, gents. How are things going?'

'I'm sorry to tell you that your husband, Crail Shaw, is dead, Mrs Shaw.'

Nancy was speechless for a moment, then she smiled. 'I know, love. Serves the old bastard right.'

'Did somebody inform you of this?'

She looked to the door of the dining room, but Evans was standing there, keeping an eye on the hallway.

'I'm sorry, but I'm not saying any more.'

'Was it Jack? Did he manage to get a message off to

you before we arrested him?'

'Sorry, son, but unless you're arresting me, I'm not saying anything else.'

'Where's Brendan?'

Nancy shrugged. 'I don't know.'

'I think you know exactly where he is,' Dunbar said. Then he looked at Evans. 'Go look for him.'

Evans walked away. Then, suddenly, Nancy acted like she'd had a jolt of electricity pass through her. She shoved Dunbar out of the way and made it to the doorway before he grabbed hold of her.

'Brendan! Run!' she screamed over and over, then the life went out of her.

Dunbar put her hands behind her back.

'I didn't know what they were doing. But they're my boys, so I'm not helping you put them away.'

'Save it for later,' Dunbar said, then shouted for the uniforms to come in. He passed Nancy over and ran up the stairs, having seen Evans go that way.

When he reached the top, he saw Evans go into his own room. When he got to the doorway, he looked in and saw Brendan Shaw standing with a large kitchen knife, pointing it at Evans.

'Get back or I'll stab this fucker to death.'

'It's over, Brendan. Don't make it worse for yourself,' Dunbar said.

Brendan sliced the air in front of Evans, making

him move round. Evans got closer to the bed, keeping his eyes on Brendan.

Brendan made another slicing motion, and then Dunbar brought out his extendable baton and snapped it open in one fluid movement. He smacked Brendan's wrist with it as the man moved in closer. Then he hit him full on in the face. Brendan dropped the knife and put a hand to his nose.

Evans moved in, grabbing Brendan's arm and kicking his feet from under him. As Brendan went down, he reached a hand out for the knife. Evans kicked him hard between the legs, then kicked the knife over to Dunbar.

'Jesus, that extendable baton thing *does* work. Who knew?' Dunbar said.

'I almost got my hand on the tennis racket,' Evans complained.

'It was almost fifteen-love for him, son.'

Uniforms rushed up the stairs and entered the room. They were soon handcuffing Brendan.

'I don't know about you, but I haven't had this much fun on holiday for a long time,' Dunbar said. 'Just a thought, though: maybe you could have a tennis racket tattooed on your arm.'

'You'd like that, eh?'

'Just a suggestion, son. But think about it on the boat home.'

'Boat?'

'There's no way I'm sitting in a wee aeroplane with you honking the fucking thing out again. It will just be me, Alex and Debbie Comb.'

'Fine by me.'

'Don't worry, I'm sure Harry McNeil will be quite happy to keep you company.'

THIRTY

A few days later

Harry was sitting drinking his coffee when Alex came into the living room.

'Morning, honey.' She leant down to kiss him on the cheek.

'Good morning. How are you feeling?'

'I'm fine, Harry McNeil. How are *you* feeling?'

'I swear to God, I don't know what was worse, the plane or the ferry. You were gone by the time the rain hit. Robbie couldn't keep anything down. Poor sod.'

'You're getting the colour back in your cheeks again.' Alex giggled. 'The plane was quicker. And I didn't see Jimmy bawling and greetin' like a bairn.'

'I have to say, this is going to affect your assessment when we get back into the office.'

'Oh, I'm sure I can persuade you to change your mind.'

'That's the last thing on my mind. And to be honest, I think for our next holiday, I want to go to a caravan, just like Jimmy's wife.'

'We'd have to get a dog.'

'Don't push it.' He got up from the table to go back through to the kitchen for more coffee.

'One thing, though: when we were on the island, you were about to tell me something before we were interrupted.'

Alex thought about standing in front of Vanessa's grave. She had thought it a good idea at the time to tell Harry. Now it seemed silly.

'It's not important. It'll keep.'

'Okay.'

They went through to the kitchen. 'In all seriousness, I was thinking about a cruise for our next holiday,' Alex said.

Harry poured more hot water into a mug after the kettle switched off.

'A cruise? Are you serious? Have you never seen the film *Titanic*...?'

AFTERWORD

Just in case you were wondering, the Isle of Laoch doesn't exist. If you look at a map of Scotland and see the shape of Tiree, and join its north and south islands, then that would be the base for Laoch. Then a smattering of Mull and you have my island. I wanted to create a fictitious island so I could make up where places were.

Point of no Return was inspired by a real-life event. If you Google The Great Mull Air Mystery, you can read all about what happened on the island back in 1975. I found it fascinating, and thought, what if...? That's how this Harry McNeil book came about.

I would like to thank my advanced reading team, and welcome aboard the new members.

A big thanks to my wife as usual, for looking after the dogs while I write. And a huge thank you to my

AFTERWORD

new editor, Charlie Wilson and her willingness to take me on as a client at short notice.

And as usual, a big thanks to you, the reader, who make this all worthwhile.

Stay safe my friends.

John Carson
  New York
  October 2020

Printed in Great Britain
by Amazon